darkness throw

may these words provide solace and consolation as always,

peter plate

darkness throws down the sun

peter plate

Polygon
EDINBURGH

© peter plate 1991

First published 1991 by
Polygon, 22 George Square, Edinburgh

Set in Sabon by Koinonia, Bury and
printed and bound in Great Britain
by Redwood Press, Melksham, Wiltshire

British Library Cataloguing in Publication Data
peter plate
darkness throws down the sun
  I. Title
  823.914 [F]

ISBN 0 7486 6117 4

The publisher acknowledges subsidy
from the Scottish Arts Council
towards the publication of this volume.

Chapter One: The Toy Store

    in the beginning a circus barker lets out a mighty roar.
    ... welcome to the finest circus on the planet today ... step this way, ladies and gentlemen ... allow your eyes to become accustomed to the dark ... step this way and do not be afraid ... this is the show that made the nation great ...
    the barker's powerful voice heightens the crowd's anticipation. a line is starting to form before the ragged entrance of the circus tent. green and blue pennants are flying in the stiff breeze while a white sky flows overhead. the ticket holders clutch the slim red cards of paper which entitle them to a free coca-cola during the intermission. they wait in line and talk about the weather.
    ... yes! the barker cries ... allow your eyes to perceive the light in the dark ... prepare yourselves for the impossible at the circus of dreams ...
    (the voice fades out)

    we start with a small death in june. the hour of desire. a terminal second. the palm of a trembling hand cups a warm breast. a man's breath is racing over pillows and sheets. his destination is a small death. he would like to achieve an orgasm. his fingers run over her nipples; the fingers never stop their circular driving motion. it is the moment when eyes shine with yearning, and the eyelids droop metal heavy with sexual hunger.
    a woman and a man. their lips meet in the summer time

behind a closed bedroom door. their underwear drops to the carpeted floor amidst whispers so low, the sentences are scuttling to hide under the bed.

. . . i can't get this bra off, she giggles, and, darling, please, could you pull down the window shade? . . . the children next door, you know.

he is on top of her. he stares down at the web of her dark hair coiling over the blankets and spilling into his hands. he is propping himself up with his elbows because he doesn't want to crush her with his weight.

. . . did you put on your rubber, ducky? she slurs the words, clinging to his chest and then drawing him to her neck. expensive perfume lingers in minute traces at the nape of her neck; the ghosts of an alluring scent. she smiles and nuzzles his unshaven cheeks with the tip of her nose. his beard prickles her skin, and she smiles again, squeezing him tighter within the circle of her arms.

. . . i don't need no rubber, babykins, he gasps, pushing himself into her. it is a miracle when she accepts him, a song without words: all of a sudden, he is there, sliding into her walls.

. . . aw, honey, she grins, the pupils of her eyes growing brilliant in their dilation . . . that feels so good.

a world without end. we die within the beat of a single breath. but if we hold it, our lungs breaking with pain, we can live forever.

they make love for a while. for how long, no one knows. the bedroom walls start to sweat. if the woman and man persist in their rocking, the wallpaper will begin to peel and crack. he tries to repress the tension mounting at the base of his spine. he does this by swallowing his tongue. it is a lesson he learned in a house of prostitution. he concentrates on controlling his tongue, bending the flesh backwards into his throat. he is waiting for her to catch up with him.

today is a celebration of peace. the war is over and the boys are returning home from enemy shores . . . we're number one, the newspaper headlines exulted. but in upstate new york, and everywhere else in the brown and exhausted hinterlands of smokestacks and mills, the tin shacks and conveyor belts dragging wet cement to the sky, women and men were already waiting for the next war to begin.

. . . c'mon, baby, will you hurry up? . . . i can't keep the seed in, he squawks.

he thinks he is going to pass out. he is a soldier boy back from combat overseas. he wants to move faster, but the need to be still tears him apart. when he comes, it is like landing with the first infantry division on the shores of an island. he bellows in her ear the words he hasn't said since childhood, rising and falling, bruising his knees until he is deaf, dumb, and blind, and then he stops, his spasms ceasing. the flood from his cock dwindles into an opaque trickle glistening on her thighs.

but she is hoping to meet him on the island . . . she runs through the jungle to the beach, running to join the soldiers on the sand. warm salt water splashes against her ankles. she looks like raquel welch in nineteen sixty six. she stumbles in the surf. the waves beat against her hips, receding, returning to the shoreline, leaving her alone with the swelling between her legs . . . help me! she screams . . . i need help!

The soldiers stand around in groups of twos and threes, smoking cigarettes. they are supervising the transportation of heavy equipment. their sun burned faces, their hardened hands bearing oil stained weapons, they watch her thrash in the surf through the lenses of their deadened eyes. she sees this and the wild green foliage of the island before a wave splashes over her. the soldiers assemble and then march into the jungle without acknowledging her (i never can say goodbye, girl). she is pulled out to sea, and there, she is drowned.

. . . that's how it is when you can't have an orgasm, when you can't come, she says later, talking. she is wearing his bathrobe and drinking a cup of strong tea. her eyes narrow over the rim of the tea cup. he is walking by her on his way to the refrigerator. he is naked and whistling a tune. the smug bastard, she mutters.

but the soldier boyfriend is not the only man in her life. she has a son by the name of little sam. he is nine years old and curious about life. he wants to give a look into the bedroom, but she tells him to go outside . . . mommy needs a rest, sam, she said, patting him on the head and smoothing his hair . . . i want you to go play in the backyard until supper time.

children with poison ivy. dogs suffering from glaring cases of ringworm. old people sitting in lawn chairs (they are resting their prosthetic limbs). the broken car on cinder blocks sprouting weeds around the fenders. the dough boy swimming pool grandpa bought last summer is turning into rubble; the cheap vinyl is cooking under the sun. the lawn stands four feet high with uncut grass in some corners while it is bald and cancerous in other places. and let's not forget the black widow spider who bit a young girl yesterday from sheer spite.

sam is searching for water in this desert. a drink from the fountain of solace would do him fine. in the neighbor's yard, the clothes-line hangs limp with shirts and towels. the lady of the house tends to the clothing, huffing and puffing, her face turning fire engine red (she's a siren when she's drunk, sam's mother says). she flings sopping wet laundry on the line, clutching some wooden clothespins between her false teeth. her arms are massive; the muscles swing loose and slack when she moves them.

she stops to look at sam while hitching her faded house frock. her gaze rests upon his face in the same way she would open a window to stare at the rain. she knows sam hit her youngest daughter on the foot with a stone after she taunted him.

. . . it was an accident, mrs lester, sam flushes . . . i didn't mean it.

. . . you are telling me a lie, young man . . . if you say three more, you will go to hell, she yells over the fence, regarding him with eyes burned hollow by embers of hate.

she dismisses him by bending over to pick up more clothes from her basket. her dress rises above her knees, her thick white legs are covered with pale blue veins. her three daughters are standing at their kitchen window murdering sam with angry words. after he hit the youngest girl, he had to fight the other daughters, keeping them at bay with a sharp stick.

a dog inserts its snout through a hole in the fence, hungry for a bite of little sam. where he comes from, nobody can say. his hair is thick despite the advent of summer. fleas and other problems inhabit the dog's matted fur. they cause him to suffer. clouds of flies hover over his martyred head, landing and taking off. his tongue is a long, black tube that drips, panting, and slobbering, the way of all things on this summer day.

sam picks up the garden hose. he sniffs it. the plastic smells hot and sick (like the upholstery of a car when the windows are rolled up). he opens the water spigot, and boiling water spurts into his face, scalding his mouth and nose ... oh god! he screams, jerking away and dropping the hose as he would a snake. he steps on it with a prayer for its immediate death. water hisses from the hose and disappears.

those are the days after the dropping of the bomb. humanity has taken a big step forward on the path of no return.

... we fried those gooks, everyone was saying in the strip of bars near tonawanda's mills. empty cocktail glasses lined the tables in the rear booths. dark and cool maple wood paneling rose above the cigarette haze. the bars were open for the pursuit of laughter, drinking beer and the clatter of money. but there was tension underlying the merrymaking: a prophesy was beginning to unfold.

... we made those gooks crawl to surrender ... thank god for the president ... he had the courage to drop the bomb ... and because of him, our boys came home.

men grow up to become soldiers. the prospects of war crash into childhood dreams without pity. conflict is the ritual performed in the absence of peace. it speeds us along the journey from birth until death without a pause. but far away from the violence of tomorrow, little sam wants to play. he wipes his face of water and hurls a pebble at the backyard fence. he has a lot to think about.

   a summer afternoon. the towns strung out along the shores of lake erie are bathing in temperatures of ninety degrees or more.
   . . . your hair is soaking wet, he says . . . and hey, could you lean over and get my fags from the night table?
   she lights up two cigarettes in her mouth and hands him one. smoking cigarettes is better after sex, they both agree, and it's good after a big meal, too.
   . . . so, what about this kid of yours? he asks her.
   . . . little sam? . . . he's no trouble . . . he's always out there playing. she exhales a jet of smoke, watching the nicotine trail vanish in the sunlight. she stubs the cigarette into an ashtray with one hand, and with the other hand she twirls a lock of hair. her fingers are deep white against the darkness of her hair . . . but i remember a time, she drawls . . . i remember when things were different . . . when life was more certain than today.
   . . . at one time i used to take sam down to the toy store in the old part of town . . . close to the railroad station where the houses have shingles made of tarpaper . . . i had some cash, and i took sam to this store that sold model airplanes and toys . . . the windows were streaked with dirt and packed solid with cardboard boxes.
   . . . it was gloomy in there, and i was uncomfortable at first . . . but this old guy with a mustache and glasses guided us through the aisles, and sam went nuts, she recalls, idly stroking her lover's arm (she recalls a perfect moment. a picture frozen in time).
   . . . and when i think back, i see the painted lead soldiers on the shelves . . . gleaming figures of martial splendor . . . the model airplanes were suspended from the rafters on invisible strings so you got the feeling they could be flying . . . motes of dust kept falling, covering everything like it was a toy store winter in the snow.

memories in the mirror of their recollection: she engaged the ageing toy store owner in talk to mark the passage of time. she entertained a lonely man with bright smiles and quips about the weather, and yes, dear god, the war was over, thank you.

sam observed the restrained quality of their dialogue, how difficult it was to say anything, and how long the desultory talk went on. he took advantage of their conversation and roamed the toy store aisles. he sang and babbled under his breath. he prised open sealed packages wrapped in cellophane. the cellophane split through the direction of his nimble fingers. plastic airplane models displayed their remarkable secrets of distance and flight to him.

. . . sam?

(the odor of airplane glue fills his nose. he inhales and hyperventilates in an effort to become dizzy.)

. . . sam? . . . come here . . . mister martin would like to show you a brand new model . . . my boy loves airplanes, don't you, sam?

(the toy store is redolent with glue fumes. is it possible the old man has left an open jar somewhere in his storage room? airplane cement is a substance capable of wreaking havoc on the human mind. the ability to perceive an object, to make the distinction between the viewer and his desire, this function diminishes under the influence of glue.)

. . . these airplanes are wonderful, aren't they, honey?

. . . they're the best gift a young boy can receive, my dear, i can assure you.

sam's mother drapes an arm over her son's shoulder, allowing a gloved hand to dangle in mid-air. she giggles, and says, excuse me, i am feeling rather odd. mister martin gazes at sam. he licks his lips like a spider ready to eat a fly. his eyes are huge and distorted behind bottle cap glasses.

. . . yes, mother, sam spouts with utter conviction . . . i'm gonna fly an airplane to africa some day.

. . . i remember sharing a chuckle with the old man by the

cash register . . . maybe it had something to do with the charm of sam's yearnings . . . the soft glue warmth putting everything where it belonged . . . the sun seemed like a letter mailed from heaven when we saw it posted in the window . . . i told sam to calm down . . . he was getting restless . . . let go of me, ma, he was whining . . . let go of me . . . you ask me about my son? . . . well, i can tell you right now . . . boredom will always be a thorn in that boy's life.

    a gothic twilight drops over the backyard. the night falls down and the day ends. sam needs to go to the bathroom, but he has to wait. in this way he is learning the law of cause and affect: whenever adults are in the picture, little sam is out of focus.
    there aren't any stars in the sky tonight. summer lightning crosses the moon, but there is nothing else. the curtains to his mother's bedroom are closed, but the window is open. the world on the other side of the window is the future. the mystery and the anger; the silence and its climax. sam listens for the laughter that presages the creaking of the bed springs.
    sex is the center of the universe. it is where some problems begin and others end. the mattress stops groaning from its job, and sam enters the house by means of the back porch. his bladder is ready to burst. but when he finds his mother's boyfriend is taking a shower behind a locked door, sam knows the world will never be the same again.
    but how his eyes did light up in the dim aisles of the toy store. his hands tore open model kits, one after another, to learn their knowledge. he wanted to absorb the magic of flight.
    he needs to fly away from the back streets. foreign territory is calling to him. foreign thoughts are beating in his heart. the child is learning to clench his fist (to feel its might), to break and seize whatever pleases him.
    unknown to any of us, sam melville is becoming a prophet of rage. he is entering the cold war years, and we hope he gets out alive.

Chapter Two

a grey streak of dawn. the last dream is in effect, and now it begins: a nightmare i cannot wake up from despite the alarm clock ringing in my ear. i interpret the rising sun to mean that i am alone in the land of my birth. when i get tired of living, i will shoot the sun; watching it fall to the rooftops below in golden shards, seeking the death of a man.
   cowboys and indians broken in the dust again. take a walk with me, baby, i have lived to see everything. a million stories have been compressed into my brain by history's pistons working night and day. i have heard the name of sam melville. praise the name and pass it on.
   but now i have changed my mind. when i rouse myself from this dead man's sleep, i will wake up screaming. the world is rotating on a razor sharp axis. everything is moving faster. i cut myself, bleeding. we are unable to praise famous men: if the president of the united states can't decide which corner of his mouth he is talking from, i will ask him to shut up.
   the future is uncertain. america's children are reminded by her ghosts that it is the end of a century. ghosts tell me, if i wake up from this killer sleep, i will never die again.

   little sam runs one more time through the days of his childhood, splashing water from pavement puddles onto his worn out black shoes. unreasoning fear drives him forward into the streets like a bullet fired from a gun. he dodges cars idling at red light traffic jams, and he skips by young mothers

pushing their baby prams down the street after a night of rain. his eyes steer him past low lying stone walls and unseen park benches. the air is fine and growing warm.
 sam notices a sandbox behind a dogwood tree in the park. the sandbox is a large rectangular thing painted red and left to fade over the course of forty years. sam dives head first into the wet sand, trying to break his fall with his hands . . . it's good practice, he says to himself . . . in case i have to jump out of an airplane.
 he gets to his feet and takes off sprinting down a gravel path. his heels kick up pieces of blue shale. he pumps his legs as hard as possible, rowing his arms like a pair of oars. he runs past a swing set that has seen better days. his lungs heave fire into his throat, tongues of fire, the breath tearing out of his mouth, and when he is ready to fly, he slams into an elm tree.
 the blood dries quickly on sam's cut lip because he is racing; the wind is annealing the wound on his face. sam moves fast without a second thought. it is a habit that will inspire him for the rest of his life.

 he comes from the anonymity of new york's steel mill districts and their outlying suburbs. life is incomplete near the shores of lake erie; nothing gets remembered there. soot stained clapboard houses with tar paper roofs dominate the landscape. the family laundry is always hanging on the line with the neighbor's steaming wash. everything smells like bleach, burned out and distant. the clothes-lines stretch to the horizon; a thousand black lines in the red dusk of twilight.
 a mother cat is walking her litter in the gutter. two grim faced men in brown overalls are changing the tires of a truck near the road's end. a white pimp with marcelled hair drives by in a fin-tailed cadillac looking prosperous. homeless people sing and shout their hallelujahs after a bowl of soup at the mission (mandatory praying is on the menu). the mercurial child slants up the avenue. he glides past the man; his long legs are taking him home to see his mother.

a quarter of a century later and a half a century high. the police had a way of recognizing sam melville in the thirty-five years of his life: pressure is a constant companion to the struggle for freedom. pressure is a garrot. once the wire is locked around the neck, the strangling begins. conflicts with authority repeat themselves. the strangling continues. after a cop knocks on your door, you can be sure he won't go away (it never ends. that's why we call this century the phase of repetition).

... i'd be happy if the police would leave me alone, sam melville will say one day ... but there is nothing i can do ... the cops have their targets ... the people they visit rather often ... and usually with the purpose of beating a suspect into pulp ... some people bleed after the first punch ... they succumb to the insistent knocking at their skulls and the rattling of their teeth ... these late night visits begin when the suspect has retired to sleep ... if you refuse to answer the policeman's summons out of cowardice or bravery, it doesn't matter ... he has a key, and he walks in or breaks down the door without being asked ... a policeman is used to having his way.

the child and the man. sam melville is lost in a dream. he is riding an elevator to the top of a skyscraper. but situations can reverse their fortunes with relative ease, and now the elevator is plunging down to the basement, hurtling through space. strips of plastic detach themselves from the compartment, whipping his back and bloodying his shirt. the lights go out, and water eddies around his feet, ruining his tennis shoes. the elevator comes to a halt. the unoiled door opens, screeching. a monstrous silhouette resembling a praying mantis fills the shaft. a high intensity flashlight is shined into sam's eyes, and he blinks. a policeman has arrived larger than life.
... gimme a cigarette, the cop belches.
... how did you know it was my last one?
... shut up, faggot. it's my business to know everything.
... if only i could wake up, sam thinks.

... forget it, the cop snaps, flicking the cigarette into the water where it dies with a sizzle ... you're an american, and there is only one way outta here, and that's when you are dead ... as long as you're cold sweating in the city, you can forget about any peace of mind ... and when you wake up tomorrow morning, i guarantee you will look ten years older, the cop says with quiet satisfaction.
   ... sam?
   ... what do you want? he snarls, turning pale.
   ... don't you know me, sam? ... (coughing and spitting) ... yeah, i guess i look sort of different now that my hair fell out ... but don't you remember me? ... i'm the guy who turned you in to the police ... i ratted on you, man.
   ... sam melville's eyes retreat into hard slits where they flash, green and blue. he has a strong nose, and if the lighting were proper, we could see his fists. he spins around to face his opponent.
   ... jesus, is that you, george? ... god, i can't believe you would have the nerve to show up again.
   ... it's the impulse to suicide, sam ... it's hard to stay away from it ... i think you know what i'm talking about, george says ... you know, you and me were big time in the news for awhile, didn't you, sam? ... it seems so long ago ... or maybe it hasn't happened yet, i don't know ... but either way, we're stars.
   sam melville growls, and it looks like he is going to sock george in the face. george's first impulse is to throw his hands over his eyes. but then he chooses to flee. however, sam is swift runner, and after several hundred yards, george's legs begin to complain. when he slows down out of breath, sam catches up with him. he plants a slap across the other man's jaw line. george spits out a tooth, and he starts to blubber.
   footsteps echo in the dark. a breeze wafts in from the waterfront flavoring the air with salt and brine. george prays for a policeman or two, but the echo belongs to a young couple walking arm in arm.
   ... oh god, can't you see? george begs in silence (as sam clamps a hand over his mouth) ... can't you see that i am a

stool pigeon? . . . i am the famous snitch known as george demmerle, and this man wants to hurt me.
. . . what's the matter, george? sam's voice travels at low volume . . . are you afraid of me? hah?
sam melville wrings george demmerle's neck. he smacks him in the kidneys a few times for extra impact. they are old friends like fucking bookends. after sam crushes george's foot under his own, forcing him to howl like a dog from hell, he twists his ear and whispers.
. . . when are you going to learn, george? . . . you are panicking as usual, and the story hasn't begun . . . how many times do i have to tell you . . . a stool pigeon never keeps his cool.

sam melville. america swallows its offspring in epileptic fits. she crushes little girls and boys in her mouth. she gags on their half-chewed remains, and having no other choice, she vomits, showering arms and legs, tattered clothes and schoolbook lessons, and spewing beautiful heads over the land. i cannot imagine which season of this century turned my country into autumn. my clothes are thin, and a harsh wind is coming. my final request goes out tonight to the kids in the neighborhood. to the brothers and sisters who have loved and hated me through the years. yes, hot lips, this song goes out to the reinvention of sam melville as a child. once upon a time, he was the flower of his mother's eye.

the year was drawing to a close. the year was getting dark. autumn's leaves fell from black and mottled trees, plastering themselves over the playground and park. the playground was empty except for a man walking his dog. he walked with a stoop, and upon second glance, he was in charge of four dogs; three more had charged into view, barking and wagging their tails. the dogs' master carried a paper bag in one hand, and a tiny red shovel was tucked under the sleeve of his goose down vest . . . quit your yapping, you goddamn curmudgeons, he yelled . . . you'd better go potty right now, he says . . . or you'll have to wait until tomorrow.

when sam comes home from playing after school, his mother is cooking in the kitchen. she wears a bandanna around her hair while she bends over the stove. she is frying a bacon and egg sandwich for her son.

. . . you spend too much time in the park, little sam, she scolds . . . it's going to make you lose your common sense.

. . . but ma, he squirmed, butting her between the breasts with his head . . . all these people are there . . . they're talking, but i can't hear a word they say.

. . . hush up, son, she places a warning finger to her lips and frowns. a thin vertical line makes its appearance on her brow . . . and put some ketchup on your egg sandwich.

under the kitchen light, his mother's head is a candle that has been sparked with a match (so bright is the kitchen in contrast to the night). her head is a wax candle, and the wick is burning down. while the wax melts, she is cooking for her son. the job of preparing food is an act of supplication. the mother is a candle, and her soul is burning down.

. . . eat your eggs, sam, and don't forget to eat the crust of the bread, too, she said, taking off the bandanna and shaking her hair . . . i don't want you growing up skinny or dumb . . . now, do your dishes and go to bed . . . tomorrow i'm gonna look for a job, and you're going to school.

Chapter Three: A Cinder in His Eye

    the neighborhood went crazy when the fire broke out. a vacant house was blowing up in a series of blue and white flames. the fire caught some telephone poles in its path. they dropped dead to the sidewalk, pulling down the power lines that got stuck in the trees while snapping off branches right and left. the windows of the house exploded. glass melted while bits of wood and plaster shot skyward into the ink black night, announcing the carnage like fireworks on the fourth of july.
    some holiday. the neighbors were screaming at the top of their lungs when the fire engines arrived. they spat and cursed, ordering their wives to be quiet while they stood around in their bathrobes by the curb. they looked no less than the sentinels of armageddon. they, too, were afraid their homes would go up in flames.
    across the street, sam's mother is sitting at her bedroom window gazing at the fire. from a certain angle, her hair reminds us of the fire: crimson stripes run the length of her tresses.
    . . . those are some pretty flames, her boyfriend mutters. now and then, he leans over to insert an exploratory hand into her open bathrobe. once there, he fondles her smooth breasts. his face is drained of color but filled with wonder. he remembers playing with fire as a kid. he recalls the urge for death that grew inside him. it was pitted against the race for sexual awakening. to make love is to die, he says. he bends over to kiss her shoulder.

he remembered it wasn't hard to reach the box of matches in the kitchen. they were on a shelf overlooking the gas stove. he discovered it was no big deal to push a chair over to the stove and mount it. his hands slip into the box where the matches are stored. blood gallops through his fingers. a river of blood pours into his brain, flooding the port of his subconscious. the travelling blood awakens the impulses buried in his head. matches are the password to danger, little stranger.

matches are the key. they are the weapons young boys use to compose the new rules. light a match; we must warm up the cold war years.

he is mad at all things. this life of never-ending school and boredom. the days and nights that hide from him, laughing at him, denying him their pleasures. he hates the plants and trees that make him sneeze. the insects that cut and sting (they cause pain when he gets stung around the eyes).

but people are the worst of all. they smell so bad, the boy thinks, it is best not to think of them . . . mom and dad . . . the next door neighbor who is a queer . . . that strange woman who tried to put her hands down his pants . . . these thoughts hurt the brain. he staggers through the kitchen and out the back door.

the law shimmers outside like cheap jewelry. his mother has a collection of fake diamonds. she calls them zircons. the lawn looks fake too. it is green for the most part, but dry and brown near the street. this is where the red ants establish their colonies. they use the dying clumps of grass as building blocks for the red ant nation.

. . . these ants, they gotta go . . . all i need is a little gasoline, he calculates.

the sun irritates his skin when he steps outside. the stench of rotting peaches is heavy in the air. the driveway is blinding hot. his temples are throbbing because his grandmother's shrill voice is combing his brain with questions: why aren't

you wearing long pants? do you want to catch poison oak? he wishes she would die, but he knows she is immortal.
   his stomach is empty. it growls, forcing wind through his tortured intestines. a bowl of corn flakes will not suffice. food cravings run wild, tending towards the berserk: he wants to set an ant hill on fire.
   the heat rises into the soles of his orthopedic shoes, scorching his imprisoned toes. he senses the death of his legs sooner than the doctor has predicted: he lurches across the lawn. the sky is a blue bowl; he wears it on his shaved head (the hair is shorn to the scalp at the barber college on a weekly basis). by the time he reaches the ant colony on the sidewalk, he is dizzy. the neighbors have stopped watering their lawns, and he is alone with his task.

   he gets down on his knees. to the casual observer he appears to be worshipping an unknown god. he drains a canister of gasoline into the ant hill door. the fluid oozes into the opening. chaos breaks out among the red ants, and they retreat, swarming in all directions. one of them clings to his leg. he yells and jumps back, smashing the ant against his shoe.
   this is the signal he needs. the catalyst he wants to feel. the surge in his groin. his fear of insects unlocks his desire for death . . . he strikes a match and tosses it onto the ant hill. the central mound with peripheral tunnels explodes into flames, singeing his socks. he steps back, and like a general waiting for the battle to end, he crosses his arms. he searches the sandy ground for survivors. he observes the results of his raid. he finds that nothing is left. the deaths of several hundred ants are on his conscience. their shadows, their feeble antennae wave across the blankness of his mind.

   fire on the night. hoarse voices ringing in the street. throats spill over with secret longings. a man stares at his neighbor's wife. fire engines with hook and ladder devices have arrived on the scene, but the fire is shredding the burning house with staccato bursts of light. the building is starting to collapse to one side; it is a discotheque wilderness of flames.

smoke pours out of the damaged house. the smoke wreathes the street with gray and black fumes, the telling signs of arson. the boyfriend is alone with his memories. the mother lives in a country stripped of everything but her thoughts. the child learns to strike a match. together, they are hypnotized by a house on fire.

. . . yes, he sighs.

. . . what did you say, honey? sam's mother holds her boyfriend's hand. she can't hear a thing because the fire engines are at work, heaving water. tonawanda's fire department better get itself some new machinery if they want to beat fires like this, she smirks . . . but if we're gonna have a fire, hell, it should take this whole damn town with it . . .

this is life trapped inside a snapshot. seize a moment and freeze it. sit down and realize you have been living in the same way the blind read braille: without seeing.

sometimes, his mother's boyfriend came over to the apartment full of laughter and cunning smiles. he would pick sam in his strong hands and throw him in the air, catching him before the child hit the floor with his head.

. . . i've got a secret, sam, and i want you to guess what it is . . . all you have to do is run into the bedroom and get under the covers . . . when i say ready, steady, go, you come back into the living room and tell me what you found.

his mother stood in the kitchenette doorway, slender and fine in a rayon dress. genuine pearls were stitched into its beaded yoke . . . you do what he says, sammy, she winked at him.

he ran to the bedroom and closed the door behind him. without taking off his shoes, he leaped onto the bed and burrowed into the blankets like a beaver. he snuggled towards the center of the mattress, inhaling the history of his mother and her lover. he identified the odor of vaseline and the more cloying tang of her boyfriend's after-shave. his hand encountered a thin film which crumbled under his touch. he waited under the covers for a long time. he counted the sheep that jumped over the fence in his brain.

the signal that would release him was never given. but sam sprang from the bed, anyway, tripping over the blankets and crashing to the floor. he lay there, blinking back the tears and rubbing his sore knee.

his mother and her lover were not to be seen, but he could hear their smothered giggles in the bathroom. he tiptoed to the door and stopped when he saw his mother hook her leg over the man's shoulder. he watched the boyfriend roll down the nylons from his mother's thigh. he saw this through a crack in the door. and then sam decided it was time to go outside.

he is wandering in the ruins. a pilgrim for our times. he is not supposed to be in the house that caught fire, but he has nowhere else to go. piles of clothes are strewn about, destroyed by fire, and wrecked by water. the gutted foundation exposes its hideous backside to the sun. overstuffed chairs hunch over their short legs, and shoes are scattered like a herd of animals. a hoover vacuum cleaner lies on its side. dust balls and orange peels seep from the torn vacuum bag. live cinders drift in the breeze, floating away, one after another. sam discovers newspapers impossible to read. ruination has covered the newsprint with trails of ashes and rat shit.

. . . what the hell are you doing in that house, kid? the old man from the brick house next door shouts . . . you'd better get out of there before i call the police on you.

sam turns around. he staggers. he's been shot in the back by a line of bitter words. he kicks a pile of cans in disgust and grimaces. the man's fierce words suffocate him; they imply a threat he can't understand (they prevent him from reaching the subject of his desires, which is desire itself). he opens his mouth to protest innocence, and a cinder flies into his left eye.

. . . oh my god! he cries . . . i can't see! . . . i can't see! . . . somebody! please! help me!

his horrified voice travelled up a chimney of agony. tears ran down his face. he wanted to find comfort, but solace was scarce during this hour. the boy's mother is behind closed doors. later, she goes to work. she will not find out about the accident until it is late in the day. by the time sam visits a doctor, the diagnosis is grim: he has lost the sight of his left eye.

the smell of iodine and the sterilizing steam from the instrument tray is keen in his nose. the doctor is moving within earshot, calling to him . . . sam . . . sam . . . this is doctor evans . . . can you hear me, boy?

sam remembers all the things he has seen. he hasn't lived long; his memories go by him very fast. he didn't think his dreams would change. he thought the flavors of the nights and days of life on earth would remain the same. but sam's journey is turning its slow wheel towards the promised land.

. . . things will be different now, sam, the doctor tells him while bandaging the injured eye with gauze pads. the florid-faced physician cuts a length of surgical tape with his scissors and remarks . . . things will look distorted for awhile, and then, they'll get clearer as time goes on . . . and if you can help it, eat a carrot every so often to strengthen your vision, okay?

one eye is bright and blue. this eye will look to the future and find trouble. the other eye is green and quiet, a blind ocean. this eye belongs to the past, to the promises we never forget, even if they don't come true. the doctor continues to banter. he offers sam an aspirin. but sam does not acknowledge him. he no longer cares where he is. no words will come from him tonight. his mouth has turned into a bar of silver.

Chapter Four

sam melville is burying his mother in a snowstorm. he is alone with a shovel digging at the frozen soil. the sub zero air destroys the brain and terrorizes warm-blooded animals into submission, but despite the temperature, sam is working in his shirt sleeves. he is too busy to feel the cold.

if he could think of something to talk about, death would interrupt sam, greeting him, saying, hello there, sam. how are you today? but sam keeps quiet, silent as a night spent in church, and death stays away.

the shovel burns his ungloved hands. the cold metal tears at the tissue. the soil is ice hard, and the snow covering the ground makes sam's task seem like a losing battle. a row of evergreen trees sway on a nearby ridge. a raging wind is flying through their sodden branches. the wind speeds over the ridge, disappearing in a moment of calm, and then it returns, twice as loud. the sun is refusing its own power today, and without the sun, this day has become a winter killing.

sam straightens up, grunting. he is weighted down by a shovel full of granite. he drops his load on a rock pile with a flick of his wrists, and then he repeats the process, slamming the shovel to the soil. the shovel rasps along the ground with a mournful rhythm (sad and heavy like clouds). he thinks about a summer day on the shores of lake erie. a day when he was sunbathing with his mother.

she was looking good in the white two piece swimsuit she wore. it wasn't quite a bikini, but close enough, he thought. the water from the lake was unpolluted, or so the newspapers said. a thin foam left midget crabs scrambling in the surf. a southerly wind blew sand over the public beach. the sand invaded everything from plates of tuna casserole to the underwear of girls. the emotions of these girls are hidden behind impassive faces. this is how they do the boy watching thing.

sam gazed at his mother. she stood up and brushed the sand from her sun-burned arms. her natural movement precipitated a certain fate she could not escape: two young fellows stopped to ogle her. the length of her legs, the tautness of her belly, and the swell of her breasts, not to mention the way she arranged her hair. the men stopped and did the appropriate thing; they craned their heads to whistle at her, taking off their sunglasses to punctuate the thrill.
life is a camera. everyone is looking (or being watched).

hot fun in the summer time. cool cat looking for a kitty. sam jumps to his feet, clutching two fistfuls of sand. he is ready to fling his arsenal of hate at the enemy. the image of his mother has been desecrated, but he will protect it.
. . . hey, ma, he yelps . . . those guys whistled at you!
. . . she indulges him with a smile . . . don't you know they're paying me a compliment, baby? she says without a trace a reproach marring her mouth. it is a mouth that gleams coral pink and inviting . . . you see, she goes on to explain, sketching a diagram in the sand with a polished fingernail . . . when a man likes a woman, especially a young man, he wants to give her a signal . . . something to alert her to his presence . . . it's a code of give and take . . . of dominance and surrender.
she stops and smiles again. she is pleased with the instructive value of her comments . . . sam is such a sensitive boy, you know, she says . . . he needs a good word to the ear now and then.
his mother walks to the water's edge. she approaches a gaggle of men drinking beer and horsing around in the yellow sand. waves are breaking at their feet. they shout with joy and

throw their beer cans into the lake. the cans roll back and forth with the tide until they are forgotten. sam watches her when she talks to a sun-tanned blonde man. but he looks away when she touches the man lightly on his bare shoulder. she is laughing at something he said. it was a flirtatious statement created in order to please her. she makes sam angry at the times when she is not mad at him.

before we remove its arms, let us move the clock forward by a few years. if we break the clock's arms, we can obtain another view of a woman and her son.
    she is sitting in the living room. she is reclining in a chair with her arms crossed. the sun is peeking in the window; the shadows it provides throws her head into dramatic relief. his mother sits in the chair, complaining about its features.
    ... it cost me sixty dollars, she fumes ... and it is ugly ... can you tell me where we can get that kind of money for furniture again? ... this chair was supposed to decorate our living room, but it turned out to be a failure, she sniffs.
    ... why don't you throw it out, ma? he ventures.
    she finds his treachery unfathomable. where does he get these ideas? but the disgust that trails across her mouth is something else: in one minute or less, he knows she will castigate him. it is a family tradition. when the parental voice supercedes the ritual of complaining and becomes the frenzy of a quarrel. in this contest, no prisoners are taken. submission is unconditional. sam gulps, and two red spots surface on his cheeks. barbed wire anger is rippling in his mother's voice.
    ... what are you talking about, little sammy rich boy? ... why are you talking like a big little man? ... and with whose money, that's what i want to know ... do you know what it's like to work all day, and then go buy a chair that you bring home to hate? ... do you understand, sam? ... it takes the blood out of your veins when you are asleep ... and when you wake up to look out the window at the smoke stacks ... looking at them sort of mesmerized ... yawning and reaching for a cigarette even before you've wiped the sleep from your

eyes . . . wondering if your husband is out there but never knowing . . . on those days when you wake up, how do you know you're alive?

one day, when she is away working uptown for the afternoon, sam cuts school and sneaks into his mother's bedroom. he glides over the threadbare turkish carpet to the oak dresser. it is the one piece of furniture that remains from her marriage to sam's father.
. . . it was a gift from your daddy, she says . . . it was the only decent thing he did for me even though we didn't stay together long enough for him to put his clothes into it . . . but sam, i'm warning you . . . he was your father, but that's my dresser . . . you keep your filthy hands off that damn thing . . . there are secrets in there, and they belong to me.
sam opens the top drawer. he removes a brown paper bag of polaroid snapshots. he discovers photographs of his father standing at attention with other men under a trade union flag. deep circles brand their eyes like they spent the entire previous night drinking whiskey and playing cards. the pictures are held together by an old rubber band that snaps and breaks in his hands. the other photographs depict people sam has never seen.
. . . your father, she informs him . . . your father is a communist . . . a lot of good it did him, she laments . . . and look at me, she laughs . . . i'm a communist's widow.
the hands of the clock stand still with our reflection. the pictures of his father fill him with rapture . . . there is somebody i look like after all, sam thinks.
get ahead, father time. get ahead and turn this boy into a man. the battle is never over between the young and old. but the clash begins in earnest a year later: sam has challenged his mother's boyfriend to combat in the dining room.
. . . why don't you leave her alone, mister? . . . you're just using her.
. . . you'd better shut your gob, sonny boy, or i may lose my temper . . . and if i do, i'll use the belt on you.

a short time later, a scuffle breaks out in the kitchen. sam lunges at the older man, spraying him with curses. he pushes him against the cast iron stove and gets ready to take a swing, but the conflict is quelled by the lady of the house.

. . . oh, you men, she flutters in between them, teasing and scolding, gauging them as they circle around each other, anticipating the next moment to pounce and exchange blows . . . now don't be stupid, for goodness sakes, she pouts . . . think of the misery the two of you are causing me.

. . . i can't take it anymore, ma . . . these guys are no good for you . . . and they keep hanging around, coming back for more.

. . . you're jealous, sam, she quips, and almost laughs (but chooses not to at this awkward moment). she murmurs something inaudible and fishes a cigarette from her purse.

. . . sam, there is nothing i can do about the way i am . . . i need a lot of attention . . . maybe if your father hadn't left us, this wouldn't be happening . . . i try to take care of you the best i can . . . but if it's not good enough for you, i just don't know what to do.

he left home the following morning after he made his bed and put a few books back on their shelf. it was noon when he left her sitting in the hated chair. cigarette smoke was curling around her head. she did not say a word when he walked out the door.

fear lances his stomach as he steps onto the porch. this is not the hour to look back, he realizes . . . maybe later when there is more time . . . he takes a deep breath, drawing it into his lungs until there is pain, and then he runs down the steps. he is boarding a bus pointed towards the east side of town.

each year ended with a new landlord and a cheap but clean rental. there were downtown cafeterias to explore in every town. sam grew up with the ham sandwiches and jello puddings you can buy for a dollar and a quarter. he learned to take refuge in public libraries; he stuck his nose into books that were ancient and smelled funny. but he couldn't stop thinking about his mother's boyfriends. they kept changing like the seasons or the cities where they lived. life was a merry-go-round; it influenced sam melville to transform the story of his past whenever he was inclined to, changing everything but the color of his eyes.

sam melville is burying his mother and her possessions in a snowstorm. some pictures escape from a shoe box and sail away on the wind. he snares one of the photographs before it disappears. he holds a dream of the past in his aching hands. it is the image of his mother.

she is smiling for the camera man. she displays a mouthful of perfect teeth and the tip of her tongue. her forehead resembles a porcelain vase, and her skin is pure honey. her lips wait for any man strong enough to endure her kisses. this is what she alludes to with a dimple on her chin. her hair is wrapped up in an embroidered scarf. the photograph is black and white, but the treated paper is turning brown. we know the picture is old, but sam melville's mother looks vital and fresh despite the passage of untold years.

he knows he loves her. but confusion interrupts his need for an uncomplicated past. a particular question never leaves his mind: should he forget the years he spent with her, or can he alter it to his convenience?

sam melville is a self-invented man. he seeks his reflection in the future that waits ahead. the weather is turning bitter cold. scraps of paper soar on the wind. pieces of white paper land like birds into the trees. sam slows down the pace of his shoveling as his arms begin to weary. he is an indefatigable man, but he must face the facts . . . i gotta get some rest, he admits.

the sun is coming up from an ocean of blood. the snow is falling harder than ever. he shivers. this is a dream where there is no sleep. after sam melville buries his mother, he is travelling to new york city.

Chapter Five: Journey of the Soul

 . . . wanna buy some acid? the man on the telephone inquired.
 . . . i don't talk about stuff like that on the phone, sam replies . . . but i'll come over in a couple of hours, and we can discuss the issue then.
 . . . right on, brother, the dealer wheezed . . . i'll see you in my cage at noon.

 sam ambles through the streets of the city. he overhears the tired conversations of the russian grandmothers sitting on their stoops. homeboys are screaming out the names of their products at the corner . . . blast off . . . blast off. . . the wet wool smell of rain is in the air again, and in sam's estimation, the soup kitchen lines are longer than ever. this thing called daily life cuts into his nose like a whiff of ether, sharp and astringent.

 (i scream. i lick my lips to sort out the breadcrumbs from the saliva. i sniff away the remains of a winter cold. i emit some kind of sound which a pedestrian takes for a beggar's request. he deposits a shiny quarter into my pocket without a glance, and then he walks away, whistling. the high noon sky hangs low over the horizon. its belly is slung like a pouch over city hall. rain pulls on the clouds, pissing in the streets below.
 i see the junkies in the alley where boxes of fruit sweat with

a waxen fever. i walk through this world like a jewish prince among fellow thieves. i see the jet planes that crash on the evening news, and when i am walking downtown, who am i to resist the advances of an aging drag queen? everyone needs to love, to kiss, and to hold hands (in the back seat of a taxi zooming through the village at dawn).

but i don't wonder about these things; i just take it as it comes. i live like a man who turns in his sleep to face the wall. i sleep like a man who remembers everything or nothing at all.)

the twin smoke stacks come into sight as sam turns the corner. he sidesteps dreadlocked bicycle messengers and the occasional police van. smoke rises from the park in thick gray columns, from fires built in fifty gallon oil drums.

. . . that acid, sam melville muses, thinking to himself as he clambers the tenement stairwell to the dealer's cage . . . that acid is going to make this week ripe for revelations.

sam has been ingesting the hallucinogenic for three months on a consistent basis. he considers the psychedelic an excellent tonic for the cold war climate boiling in his head. acid does away with the limits. it's an effective method for fighting depression. in czechoslovakia the drug is utilized to cure patients of chronic dipsomania. by the time sam reaches the dealer's apartment, he is full of himself and ready for anything. he knocks on the painted door with his usual fervor.

the door opens immediately. a sallow-faced man with stringy hair glares at sam . . . do you have to hit the door so hard, brother? . . . you're gonna bring the heat down on me that way, the dope man whines.

. . . but i got that good acid, he tells sam . . . i got some choice double dome . . . it's purple like the moons surrounding the planet venus . . . you hear what i'm saying?

the dope man escorts sam down a dank hall into a dwarfed living room. the room is furnished with the typical village decor of lawn chairs and milk crates. sam steps over an open can of dog food. through the closed windows he can feel the late winter chill.

. . . shit, i don't know if today would be a good day to trip after all, sam confesses. he rubs his hands to ward off the cold.

. . . no, no, no, man, the dealer exhorts, refuting sam with an authoritative smile that breaks his face into a million fine lines . . . today is the best day to take this acid of mine . . . this is clean acid . . . it's not the same white bitch who could get you strung out on caine.

. . . if you and i drop some tabs, the dope man persists . . . it would be a good thing, believe me, you.

. . . i don't know about that, sam frowns, stern and serious . . . i was thinking about buying a hundred hits from you . . . but i was going to take them later . . . you know what i mean?

. . . you gotta trust me and my product, the dope man says flatly . . . i know what's best for you, he adds, looking sam dead center in the eye before he utters the magic word . . . brother.

the logic of brotherhood puzzles sam. neighborhood culture of recent invention has set up the dealer as an indisputable icon. not only is the dope man the distributor of mind-bending products, he is also a signifier. he is the latest code. he provides dope and the word. sam would prefer to buy now and consume later. but he finds there are compromises to be forged between him and the other.

. . . all right, dope man, sam announces . . . you're right.

sam is proud to conquer his doubts. this minor triumph deserves recognition: he suggests they each swallow four tabs. the dope man flinches. four hits? fuck, he mumbles to himself, i'm gonna be climbing the walls.

but to sam's face he says . . . good idea, man . . . i'll go heat up the instant coffee.

the dealer stirs the coffee grains around in their cups. he would offer milk and sugar to sam, but he doesn't have any. he twirls a spoon in one cup and then the other. the dope man is tired. more people are questioning the efficacy of his role by the day. he is dazed by the struggle to retain his post, the top notch groove in the realm of contraband.

. . . it's getting to be a bitch convincing the brothers and sisters about my importance, he says without rancor.

he's not angry. if the dope man doesn't remain philosophical about the ups and downs of life, who will?

the acid is stored in three refrigerators . . . you gotta keep the stuff chill, or it gets weak on you, the dealer explains . . . this shit doesn't have a long shelf-life . . . that's why i gotta keep it in a refrigerator to make sure it stays strong.

he never tires of gazing into the refrigerators . . . there's my babies, he croons. he will never fail to enjoy the uniform beauty of the purple tablets stored in their plastic cylinders. a white sticker is adhered to the top of each cylinder. the digits three, zero, and seven are stencilled in red letters to every sticker. this figure refers to the number of micrograms each tablet contains . . . it's enough to blow the brains out of godzilla, the dope man grins.

they drink their coffee and swallow their tabs. after thirty minutes of anticipation (the tension threaded through the two pin-rolled reefers smoked in ceremonial silence), the acid hits sam. it has the impact of a railroad train hitting a dog on the tracks.

sam looks up, startled. not only is his head rocketing through the ceiling, but the roof is lifting off, as well. it must be a hurricane, he reasons with his last sober thought.

. . . cars are overturned by seething winds. crying children whimper in city cellars. lightning rips into the trees, shattering branches and calling out unknown names, the devil in the electricity. the sky roils black at its vortex, undulating in shock waves over the power lines. the walls of the dope man's living room begin to conspire against sam. they close in. by three o'clock the walls will be the size of a match box, and he shall be no larger than a shirt button. the knowledge saddens him. he staggers to the living room window, but when he gets there, the window disappears. (he sees a plane overhead. the pilot smiles and waves at him.) . . . ah, fuck, this is getting

heavy, he groans.
. . . hey, dope man, he blurts . . . you got a bathroom i can use? . . . i wanna go look at my face . . . something is starting to eat away at it . . .
sam walks down the narrow corridor searching for the bathroom. dense cobwebs block his movement. he taps the walls ahead of him like a blind man. he tries to avoid colliding with the cream-colored walls. they are cool and moist, resembling the skin of an unhealthy man. he finds the bathroom. but the moment he enters the chamber, the exposed toilet plumbing wraps itself around his ankles and sucks on his shoes . . . christ, what's happening? he howls.
and then he sees himself in the mirror. no other lost continent, no star-studded galaxy could have blown his mind more than the sight of his own flesh dissembling and rearranging itself as well. he steps closer to the mirror. the planes of his jaw shift with the flexing of the tendons. his blue eye is framed in a bubbling vessel of red skin. his green eye is a jewel. it sags a few inches outside of the socket, gleaming at the end of two pink ligaments.
sam opens his mouth. thirty yellow fangs pop into view. sam closes his mouth. the skin stretches so tightly over his chin, he can see the bones underneath. he marvels at the structure of his skull. he runs a hand over his hair, and when he closes one eye, he notices his forehead is lopsided. he hears a mild knocking at the bathroom door.
. . . who is it? he asks.
. . . it's only me, sam . . . it's only me . . . only me, someone echoes.
sam pokes his head into the hallway. he peers through the gloom in both directions. the dim light provides him with few clues. he listens to a radio droning somewhere downstairs. the bass and treble are coming up through the floorboards. he can taste the instant coffee in his mouth, the way the sour aftertaste digs into a big cavity.
. . . it's only me, sam . . . only me.
. . . what do you want? sam gnashes his teeth, spitting. his hair is raised on end. he presses his back to the wall and lashes

out, kicking with both feet. but to no avail. he is a prisoner. a terrible satin darkness falls over his head choking him, and he screams. a cold tremor passes over his left shoulder: sam melville has become acquainted with death. he will never forget the smell.

. . . i am pleased to meet you, young man, death cackles . . . may i shake your hand?

. . . brother . . . brother . . . what's all this noise . . . why are you being so uncool in my cage? the dope man's indignant voice knifes sam in the heart . . . you could get me busted with your static . . . you hear what i'm saying?

sam needs a miracle. he is breathing in short, harsh gasps. the hallucinogenic he imbibed did not prepare him for a rendezvous with eternity. he leans on the dope man's proffered arm and takes one step at a time back to the living room.

. . . i saw death in your bathroom, man . . . i swear it! he yells.

. . . listen, the dealer growls . . . turn down the volume, or i will have to turn you out into the cold and uncaring street . . . do you know where i am coming from?

. . . this is some bad shit, sam melville whispers . . . i swear, i saw death in your goddamn bathroom.

. . . what do you mean, this is bad stuff? the dope man's words mock sam. his voice is smooth and reptilian hard . . . this is the finest product in the city right now . . . people have been banging on my door all night and day for a taste of this fine stuff.

the dope man zeros in for the kill with lyrical cunning. the sight of acid-shocked sam whets his appetite for mayhem. he licks his lips and snaps his fingers, savoring his skill in the art of double talk . . . but here i am, saving some of that precious double dome for my brother, sam, he sings . . . now you can't tell me this acid of mine is bad news, can you, sam? . . . tell us the truth, my little friend, the dope man chides.

. . . but i saw death, sam melville insists.

. . . brother man, the dealer's retort pins sam's head to the wall . . . death is in the eye of the beholder . . . if you want it, he will come for you . . . now why don't you get your ass out of here . . . i got some business to take care of.

the dealer is hallucinating dragons and snakes, sam melville looks like frankenstein to him. but he is not worried (he's got some valium in the medicine cabinet). he opens the front door after unlocking it and points to the stairwell with his hand.

sam rushes out the door. he doesn't procrastinate, and he won't dawdle. ambivalency has never been a problem for him. the dope man watches sam's back recede down five flights of the stairwell. on a late winter's day, the rivers are beginning to thaw. green buds are erupting on the bare limbs of trees. spring is not far away . . . and there goes my brother man, sam, the dope man says with a smile. he closes the door to his cage. he wonders who will be next in line.

Chapter Six: Babylon Is Burning (Red House)

the city is burning with anxiety. the streets constitute a raw nerve; stripped naked and branded by the imprint of a billion footsteps. news vendors curl up inside their kiosks, staying away from the sun. they are waiting for a shipment of the afternoon news. a black teenager was shot and killed by a mob of white kids last night, and the morning headlines were screaming murder.

a municipal bus halts for a red light. the passengers refuse to look at each other during this spell. a furtive glance, a stray gaze like a sniper's bullet can produce unexpected results. the flick of a stiletto drawn from its sheath or a derringer removed from a vest pocket: don't move a muscle, jack, and you may get off this bus alive.

let us set the mood straight. there is tension in this house. the city is where the dead walk with the living. sleepwalkers are everywhere. a man sits on a sidewalk bench wearing newspapers stuffed into his sleeves. he cradles a radio in his arms just like mother mary holding the baby jesus in that godawful manger. tunes spill from the radio's speaker, regaling the listener with forty thousand watts of longing... only in america can a poor boy like me fall in love with a rich girl like you...

success. what happens if you don't achieve it during your lifetime? magazine articles are claiming the city's potential for homicide is increasing. the police should do something about it before the course of history is changed, they say.

the city is a labyrinth. it is organized into a system of riddles that must be solved. first, you must choose to be rich or poor. the poor man is an outlaw in the eyes of society. sometimes, he carries a gun. the rich man is a good citizen. he wears a bullet proof vest and plans for an early retirement.

    the choices are not secrets. twentieth-century man, take a look at the deck of cards waiting to be shuffled. close your eyes and pick a card: now you can gamble with your life. the city is on fire. demons are coming out of their closets. they are running into the streets brandishing torches. life will change, the demons are fond of saying.

    sam melville is strolling near the park in a foul mood with nothing to do. the city looks at him from windows that are broken, and from buildings abandoned twenty years ago. other tenements rise up from the carbon mist. laundry steam and garbage smoke marry each other on the rooftops. they give birth to an unending skyline haze. radios blast out super cool songs in praise of women and money . . . life ain't nothing but bitches and money . . . ten thousand radio stations are conquering and dividing the sanity of a nation.

    scavengers and tin-can collectors examine the trash in the gutter. they stab mounds of clothing, dishes, broken tools, diapers, and syringes with long poles constructed for the task. once in a while, they find an arm or a leg zipped up in a garment bag. the human body is an ornament used and manipulated to express a variety of emotions. but the sight of a severed limb is an omen no one likes . . . it's a bad sign, the street people mutter, crossing themselves, and finishing off a quick prayer by kissing their thumbs.

    even though it is morning, boredom grows in sam melville's eyes. it is a couple of weeks before spring, and he is depressed. in these last days of winter, the sun floats over the city like a junkie with a wounded arm. the sun is searching for sam, but he is impossible to find.

    . . . damn him, the sun growls. it withdraws into a bank of

clouds, causing the city to subside into a breath-taking hush (flocks of pigeons rise in alarm and take wing across the neighborhood) . . . i know he's out there somewhere looking for trouble . . .

but when his friend jane asks him to explore the cause of his depression, he fails to explain the emotion in coherent terms.
. . . i don't know why i'm like this, doll, he puts his arms around her . . . that's just the way it is, sometimes, because i'm living in the jungle.
jane tries to disengage herself from his caresses. she knows he would rather kiss her than talk . . . it's a sweet trait, she confides in a girlfriend . . . but it doesn't change a thing, she says.
. . . listen, sam, she fumbles in his arms, twisting around so she can look into his eyes . . . you've got to figure out what you're doing . . . you said it best the other day . . . there is no time to lose.
jane is a decade younger than sam. she is younger but wiser. the difference in their ages enables her to see the cold war scars that sam wears without recognition. the cold war is a winter overcoat that sam has forgotten to take off after the months turned into summer. sam is a survivor who doesn't know how to live. but jane believes in the will to power. some memories crush passion to pieces. but jane would like to help sam remember the past without nostalgia.
on a full moon, the death wish of his generation will cross over his face when the light is right. the wish is a shadow endowed with human features. what's that? sam will ask.
. . . it is the face of your own death, sam melville . . . passing by your shoulder to let you know it is coming.

sam is taking a bath in the kitchen tub. he ducks his head underwater, sputtering and spewing bubbles. jane is perched on the tub's rim. she is throwing cold water on him from time to time. he is an unconscious man. but how long will he be able to get away with it? the crossroads where he stands is the

same for every twentieth-century man: he is returning to childhood dreams, or he is waiting in line for oblivion. every woman and man stands alone until she or he chooses to fight for the rights of others. alienation is the bullet in sam melville's gun. but he has a tendency to point the weapon at his own head.
. . . i've got to do something, jane, because there's a war going on.
. . what war is that? she asks
. . . the war for my mother's love, he answers in a rare burst of candor.

time. is it a cuckoo clock? or is it the pages of a calendar marking the days until we cross over into unknown territory? it is time to ride the dragon, sam. that's what time it is.
. . . poor sam, jane sniggers . . . you are capable of tearing down tall buildings with your bare hands . . . if you could only decide which one you wanted.

that night jane wakes up to find sam staring at the ceiling. sleep is an ocean, and you want to swim in its warm waters all the way to the equator. when you get there, you crawl exhausted to its shores. sleep is an ocean, but the shore doesn't have a harbor.
she rubs her eyes, and without thinking, she taps sam on his chest. he twitches with her touch, but nothing more. street lights cast phantoms on the bedroom curtains. sam watches them travel over the ceiling to the floor. he starts to talk automatically.
. . . i was always taking off . . . i would leave the classroom when the teacher wasn't looking . . . running across the playground . . . i believed that i had wings . . . even when the second grade teacher came up behind me and yanked me by my ear back to the classroom . . . and even when she made me stand for three hours in the hallway as punishment, standing inside a chalk circle . . . i still believed i had wings.

jane listens to sam until he falls to sleep. memories hang from his brain like bats in a barn. after the sun goes down, the bats whizz around the barn, dive bombing the horses corralled there. the bats swoop in to bite their flanks. they would enjoy a mouthful of blood.

a late model white sedan prowls the streets these day. it is the car of choice for undercover cops working in the city. gangsters, vagrants, and anarchists come and go like the butterflies in spring. but the police are nothing less than the mountains: they are permanent. each cop toils for twenty years and then hangs up his badge and gun for a pension. unlike their enemies, they never break down. a cop never forgets who you are.

. . . good evening sam, the driver of the white sedan says . . . how are you this evening?

the cop's face is a monolith of ruby-lit flesh glowing in the dark. sam doesn't recognize the policeman. it scares the crap out of him. he moans in his sleep. jane kisses him on the neck, comforting him.

this is a dream, sam melville. but it could be life. you'd better run while you can.

the next day finds us shooting pool in a downtown bar. after the third game we are requited by the sounds of a police siren. the electronic horn seems distant at first, and then it becomes clearer: the siren is headed straight for the bar.

a cop car swerves around the corner on two tires and pulls up to the curb. a black policeman sits in the car, gunning the engine. a white cop leans out of the passenger window. he is holding a photograph in his hand. he yells at the group of men lounging near the bar's door. they are trading jokes, capping on each other, and throwing quarters against the wall. they know the cop is calling to them, but they try to ignore him. if they don't pay him any attention, maybe he will go away.

. . . hey, any of you guys recognize this fellow? the cop

bellows. he is sick with the idea of asking these low-life types for help. the black and white picture he clutches in his hand is a photograph of sam melville. it was taken from the october nineteen seventy-one issue of life magazine.

sam melville has become a poster boy for the federal bureau of investigation.

. . . yeah, we've seen him around, a guy on crutches replies, spitting out flecks of tobacco with his tongue . . . but he ain't here now . . . and i'm sure you can understand why, the man says, his words hard and flat like a spatula . . . because in our story, you see, the criminal always gets away . . .

sam melville became a man whom the media dubbed as the mad bomber. the newscasters have replaced text book historians as the archivists of our country. sam says he bombed buildings related to america's war efforts in foreign countries. current events are an organization of ideas that must be wrested away from the conformity threatening to overwhelm it. who is telling the truth? or does it matter?

. . . more importantly, we are questioning the validity of truth as a concept, says sam melville.

watching the newscasters on television is a perfect theory in practice: language is failing to change life. private misery remains the most public secret of all.

. . . and that's why i started bombing, he adds.

in america, contradictions and antagonisms co-exist. they live together without any pretense of a false unity. and without the burden of a singular truth, for he moves in many ways for a number of reasons, sam melville is going to find his solution in contradictions: he fights death with his life.

Chapter Seven

   let's look inside the window of paranoia: don't be surprised if paranoia returns the gaze. wherever there is misfortune and unhappiness, paranoia is playing its game. the police roam the streets dressed like malevolent angels in leather. they are hungry to make a fresh arrest. the look in their eyes is made sharper by the teeth of their smiles. but somehow, the gangsters always make bail when they are arrested. they try to get out of jail as soon as possible because the gangster needs to work seven days a week. and the citizens? they walk with careful, measured steps to stay out of harm's way.

   . . . it's my job to make people talk . . . give me twenty minutes with a complete stranger . . . and i'll have him spilling his guts just like that, george snaps his fingers . . . there is something about me that makes you want to confess, he boasts.
   george demmerle is a plainsclothes informant for the city's police department. he pursues his foes in various disguises. he wears their clothes and mimics their jargon. he has immersed himself in the political subculture that is sweeping america. george demmerle is a sworn enemy of communism.
   . . . but, hey, man, i like to smoke weed, george explains . . . i don't give a fuck if they're communists . . . that weed gives me a fine buzz.
   however, there are limits to george's skills. his charade as a member of the american new left possesses a peculiar flaw:

george does not like acid. in fact, he is terrified of the substance. if he ingests the psychedelic in any amount, his inclination towards trickery will dissipate. plus, george has a big problem. he is older than most of the radicals he associates with. it is a factor that dismays and puzzles him.

. . . they tell me things would be different if i took acid, george goes on to say . . . but acid makes me say words i need to hide . . . it makes me think about myself instead of my job.

like sam melville, george demmerle's consciousness belongs to the ruins of the cold war years. he remembers watching general eisenhower on his parents' console television. the television was encased within polished fake mahogany and brass-plated trimmings. it was the first television in the neighborhood. his parents were proud of themselves.

george is feeding the family dog milk bone biscuits. they are watching the program together. the dog's inquisitive eyes try to focus on the image but fail. he's a german shepherd named king. george gives him a biscuit and then he nibbles on a biscuit, too. whenever general eisenhower paused in his speech for a drink of water, george kicked king in the ribs. the dog rolled over on the throw rug and whimpered.

. . . don't you eat more of these dog biscuits than me, king, george threatens the bewildered animal . . . or i'll get real mad.

george won't take acid. he is a policeman who hates communists, but he loves to wear their clothes. george is having an identity crisis. the cold war years have laid his soul to waste. maybe if he got laid the dilemma would ease. but no one wants george.

. . . not unless he takes acid, the kids point out . . . why should we screw this guy if he won't trip with us?

. . . i had a bad trip a couple of years ago, george ventures in self-defense. he inserts the comment into a lull in the debate.

. . . you're lying, george, snaps one of the athletic young women he covets . . . you're lying and you won't trip . . . because of that, you don't get any from the sisters . . . do you understand that, you jerk?

george nods his head. but he doesn't listen to the criticisms they fling at him. what do they know, anyway? he is too busy day dreaming. it would be nice to screw one of these girls the way he'd like to, he muses, with her face down into a pillow, and with him working his body like a piston over her hips, whispering, baby, baby, baby . . .

. . . what's your name? he asks.
. . . it's not important, she smiles. she regards the confusion on his face. the woe etched into his mouth. her eyes glitter. she reaches for him . . . don't worry about it, she grins.

she puts her hand between his legs and presses. george looks over her shoulder and imagines (with his eyes closed) a vast brown field of grain. a liquid sky masses with jagged clouds calling for rain. in between the earth and the sky, a solitary tractor with a man astride it plows the soil.

the woman toils over george. his pants are around his ankles. she pumps him with her hand. she frowns in concentration. her forearm stands out muscular and taut as her hand goes up and down. george thinks about the harvest in the fields and the fiery sensation in his balls.

but now the woman who is giving him a hand is disappearing. such is the power of day dreams. the blue eyes in her tanned face are vanishing. the fields in the distance are changing color. rain starts to drop from the clouds above. the man on the tractor stands up in his seat and removes his hat. rain plasters his thin blond hair to his scalp. lightning bolts crackle and land around the tractor. the farmer waves his hat at george.

george cries like a rabbit stuffed into a hutch. the rain gives way to a tidal wave of water drowning the land. the water covers him . . . he turns around and comes back up for air, struggling to break the surface . . . and he wakes up from his nap to find a puddle of semen is drying on his stomach.

. . . jesus christ, george demmerle grimaces . . . what a fucking mess. he sits up on the couch, and when he is sure no one is observing him, he wipes his member clean with a cushion.

somehow, george does not resonate with the idealism of this new generation. he is not wild in the streets. he is not an angry young man. nor is he capable of devising a revolutionary critique of modern life. george belongs to country taverns and cheap draft beer. the bleached-blonde women who smile when he tucks a dollar bill into their push-up bras. george would belong to the pelvic thrust (let's fuck to the music) revolt of elvis presley, if he belonged to any rebellion at all.

. . . drugs are diminishing my skill to act in an effective manner, he writes to his superiors at the albany office . . . if i am to pursue covert operations among dissident elements, i am obliged to adhere to their code of drug consumption and casual sex . . . i find myself suffering from fatigue and dissimulation . . . i don't know how long i can go on . . .

the albany office has advised george to attend a rock music festival occurring in the month of august. george is dreading the assignment. it will be a test of his authenticity. he will run the gauntlet of truth . . . every major acid head in the nation will be there, he informs his commanding officer . . . and i must prove that i am one.

. . . do your job, george, he was ordered . . . we'll give you one hundred dollars a day for any information you can provide . . . plus the bus fare to get there.

. . . do i have to go by greyhound bus, sir? . . . with the smell of cigarettes, tampons, and lysol in my nose all the way from new york city?

. . . yes, george, that is how you will get to woodstock, the chief replies.

woodstock. far´ from the maddening crowd. it has been raining for a day. the area surrounding the stage is a sea of mud. thousands of mud-caked women and men are wandering in the pastures, muttering, it's beautiful, man. no one has died yet, and no one shall. in retrospect, this fact becomes larger than life at woodstock. it is a victory over logic.

george stares at the women and tries to ignore the men. he is handing out leaflets at the new york crazies table. for the occasion, he is sporting a purple football helmet and a flowing cape. he converses with anyone who cares to chat. but the other crazies leave him alone . . . his vibes are too weird, they say to each other behind george's back.

. . . brothers and sisters! . . . get it together! he wails.

george's head is swelling up with a heat stroke inside the football helmet. and without a doubt, the music is killing him. it is where his suffering begins at woodstock: george can't stand loud music. the sound system amplifies the bass guitar notes in subsonic blasts that loosen his bowels. amplified feedback scorches his ears. when sam melville meets george demmerle at the crazies table, they have established an unspoken rapport: they think woodstock is hell on earth.

sam melville is walking in the rain. he enjoys the moisture. he rubs the warm drops into his skin. he is deep in contemplative thought when he saunters over to the crazies table. george sizes sam on the spot. the stranger is older than the sea of adolescents staring at the stage. maybe if george is lucky, he can wheedle some information from sam. george lacks native intelligence, but he has traded in his ignorance for a utilitarian cunning.

. . . and that's right, he babbles, starting to make his play for sam with magnetic intensity . . . only a revolutionary can understand what i'm trying to say . . . look at this shit, he sneers, flinging an arm outward to express his supreme contempt . . . look at this pitiful scene . . . these people are nowhere . . . they are delaying the movement . . . and do you want to know why? george squints at sam, his mustache twitching inside the purple football helmet . . . it's because they take too much acid, man.

sam melville turns livid. his arms dangle at his sides. he

looks down at the ground, at the leaflets, the cigarette butts and the mud, and then he scrutinizes george, his eyes burning under hooded lids.

george recoils. he frets about his choice of words. he hopes he hasn't made a mistake . . . i didn't mean it like that, brother, george ingratiates himself with a discolored smile . . . what i meant to say is that acid should be taken after the work is done, and not before we have begun . . . you see what i'm saying?

. . . i agree with you, sam melville laughs . . . i don't like acid, either.

a fraternal moment is shared. but it's not a big deal. the signature of the masculine code is written when they shake hands. but the circumstances seem forgettable enough. however, george demmerle wants more. he notices sam has a blind eye.

george knows something. he detects under sam's easy smile the poor boy without a father who came to school wearing worn-out clothes. george commands malice like an army. he is able to injure those less fortunate than him. and, sam, he is the opposite: the poverty of his past has left him with a thin skin. he is vulnerable to everyone.

it is a basic question of power (or who will be in control). george wants to put sam in a sling, so to speak, and the task is finding out how. time may be slipping away, but the rules don't change. a stool pigeon knows his target, and sam is george's man.

. . . i bet i can press this guy's button, george broods . . . i know where he's coming from . . . i can smell it on his sleeve.

. . . how do i know you're as radical as me? george demmerle challenges sam melville in the rain at woodstock . . . how do i know i can trust you?

the rain keeps coming down and soaking the land. automobiles and trailers, inner tubes and litters of puppies are sinking into the silt and mud. photographs are shot for the newspaper back in the city. the photographs record the images of women and men bathing nude in ponds where cows come to shit and drink. the photographs will shock the country. newspaper headlines speculate: is this the creation of a new nation? or is it the same old thing without any clothes on?

unseen in the crowd, the noise threatening his sanity, george demmerle sneaks another quick glance at sam melville. the music is ringing in their ears. it is coming from the oversized stage in sheets of raging volume. half deafened and hungry, sam melville and george demmerle wink at each other in the creeping night and smile.

Chapter 8: The Hand Grenade

the news reporter turns to his co-anchor, he turns to face the nation after adjusting his tie. she shuffles a sheaf of documents, contributing a prim smile while batting her eyes. he smirks into the camera and says . . . hello in there . . . is anybody home? . . . it's time for the evening news.

it doesn't matter where we are. from the slums of roxbury to the dakota reservations, from the stucco wastelands of compton to the missile silos in iowa, we are waiting for the six o'clock report to begin on forty million television sets across the land.

the month is september. the smog clinging to the skyline is a serial murderer in disguise. everyone is coughing up huge green lungers to relieve the constriction in their lungs. there are ill tidings in the sky, but if i put on my sunglasses, i can't see a thing. i do this and then i hawk up a lunger.

dark secrets are weaving out of control. boredom. sexual frustration. leisure culture is in a state of decay. the miss teen america pageant is taking place tonight. the city is seething with high temperatures and cheap weapons. september's moon waxes for criminal activities; you can be sure somebody is going to get their ass smoked at midnight. no activity is too extreme. on the contrary: a supercession of the american dream is now in order, the news claims.

the death of black panther leader huey p. newton draws out the truth of our condition like poison from a wound. a mourner at his funeral on a hot day in the city reminds us that 'we are not winning, but we are not quitting, either . . . '

a number one radio hit in southern california tells us 'to break out the guns and ammunition because the revolution is here, and you know that it's right . . . '

in september, young and old go back to school. some students attend vocational institutions. they learn to fix lawn-mowers and washing-machines. these students are on parole from prison. others go to the christian academies where they study the bible. but the majority of us, we go back to public school.

the afternoon sun is hot during the third week of the month. the heat leaks a gold haze through the classrooms' unwashed windows. the air is saturated with car exhaust. the students' faces are ashen and gray. when the bell rings for lunch, the special education classes are let out of their rooms into a separate court-yard. they are led away from the prying eyes and the sarcastic gibes of the normal.

the cripples and the blind and the mongoloids dress in a flagrant disregard for fashion. you stare at them through a chain-link fence. the blind kids and the retards have been left behind by the prefabricated youth rebellion. they wear tragic polyester dresses and ersatz denim. they don't shop at the cool secondhand stores after school. the thrift stores line the street where your girlfriend's father sells new and used cars. thinking about her gives you a headache. you light up a cigarette. you have not tried to date rape her yet, and it's causing complications.

. . . he must be a queer, everyone gossips . . . because she's the best-looking bitch in the school from the knees up to her waist, man.

welcome to september. some of the handicapped kids

possess bodies adorned by leg braces. the braces seem to come undone at inappropriate moments: in the hallways when the cheerleaders are preening like virginal porno queens, and worst of all, the braces stir up controversy on the dance floor. the disabled kids are always herded around the school grounds by a snotty teacher's aide who raises his voice, screeching . . . rupert . . . rupert . . . wheel yourself back into line.

   these kids have strange names. but for some reason, the tyranny of public school does not bother them in the way it destroys you. you suspect something unusual is occurring. the kids nodding and rocking back and forth, some of them with drool hanging from their chins, their attendants ignoring them, their wasted legs tucked into wheelchair seats, a catheter drooping from the untucked shirt of another, the blind sister and brother holding hands of the swing set, talking to each other while facing opposite directions, the smog as thick as paste (it seems to have been squeezed out of a tube), these kids have earned your respect.
   sweat drips from your neck onto the collar of your cool shirt. the school bell rings, drilling you in the back, and shortening your life.

   your girlfriend comes up to you and puts her arms around your waist. she is pretty and healthy. her slim brown legs with their fine muscles gliding under the skin, the mischief in her hazel eyes, and the house keys swinging from her finger-tips, all of this is an invitation to paradise. but why does it leave you feeling cold and diseased with anger bubbling out of every hole in your body?
   the boys and girls with their electric wheelchairs spin around in the dirt, shifting the gears on their chairs from first into reverse. they are raising school-yard dust with gusto and glee. three blind kids stand under the shade of a eucalyptus tree, talking about the voices they hear, and the smells those

voices bring to mind. their laughter drifts towards you, riding the current of a breeze scented by geraniums, a flower that you hate. you strain against the fence, longing to receive their laughter. your girlfriend is insulted. she stamps her feet in a bad temper. before the week is out, she will have a new boyfriend, some dude named dennis. alienation is eating you alive. it is contagious, and you have infected her with the virus.

another event is taking place on this september day. a friend of yours and mine is travelling to new york city. he ought to hurry. time is running out. go man, go.

our friend allows his arm to rest in the open window. he glances to his right, and everything he sees while driving along the bridge is underwater. shallow waves are lapping over rusting cars and sunken row boats. the water isn't deep. it rides along with a gentle movement, dragging plants and fish in its wake. he flicks the radio on with a twist of his wrist. static booms from the back seat speakers. the bass is loud and treacherous. the treble is deft and mean. music angers him. it colors his driving.

without thinking, he veers into the right hand guard railing. wrenching the wheel, he steers the automobile back towards the center line. the white lines disappear under the car's wheels, mile after mile.

the sun is an escalator in the sky. it moves up and down in the reflection of his mirrored sunglasses. the car is a convertible. the car is a thermometer (the red line of the speedometer is going higher). he presses his foot to the accelerator and steps on the gas. flies smash into the windshield. he peeks into the rear view mirror: it's like seeing history itself. the bridge and the highway dissolve into a white hot needle point. the highway sinks into a glimmering mirage.

he returns to the rear view mirror for a glimpse of his face. he hasn't shaved for a week, and his knife scars stand out. they criss-cross his chin and lips. they never healed.

the bridge is an endless terminus. it may take a week to cross it. but he doesn't worry; he'll just drive faster. he pumps the gas pedal, thrilling when the speed hits ninety miles per hour or more. the wind tears at his eyes. he throws a hard look to the other side of the front seat.

his girlfriend is slumping against the padded dashboard. her hair is winding down in streamers to the floor. her dress is pulled high on her thighs. they expose nylons that have seen better days (what with all the nail polish she uses to seal the holes). her shoes have fallen off, displaying the slim lines and elegant toes of two dirty feet. she is handsome in a quiet way despite the pallor of her cheeks.

she doesn't notice the scenery on this day near the end of indian summer. she doesn't see the long highway, the pelicans skimming the water-line's surface, hunting for fish, and the starlings that flit. she doesn't see her boyfriend's neutral expression, the complete lack of emotion on his face, and it's not surprising she doesn't see a damn thing, either, because this woman has been dead for two days.

he could drive off the bridge and crash. but he's come too far for that. he howls and jacks the gas pedal. he drives forward into the sun while the radio issues disco hits from the year before. i think you know the driver's name. his razor thin teeth and gouged out eyes. and where is he going in such a hurry? death is traveling to meet sam melville in new york city.

. . . i'll see you there, he utters without a smile . . . and don't be late.

sam melville wipes his forehead with a linen handkerchief. he is participating in a peace rally near the gates of a military installation. according to historians, it is the last demonstration he will ever attend.

the sun is orange and blazing. it seduces the crowd, and they don't know it. there are several hundred people carrying banners and chanting slogans at the front doors to the installation. some demonstrators are marching in a circle while holding hands. others are playing acoustic guitars and singing songs. dragonflies zip through police barricades. phalanxes of gas-masked policemen are standing at attention. it is hard to tell whether they are dead or alive.

in sam's opinion, the protest is counterfeit. its currency has proven empty when held up to the hard light of scrutiny. the tactics of protest have forfeited their right to criticize society. demonstrations have become a symbol of sentimentality. demonstrations and protest entail unending debate. but sam is tired of talking. he has compressed himself in the center of what he knows, to the bottom of his mind, and now he wants the center to explode.

there is a sense of mystery surrounding this tall and muscular man. certain people are starting to take an interest in him. the federal bureau of investigation has opened a file on him, and soon, he will be a member of a national guerrilla organization. but the events leading up to this moment are mere fragments in time and place: sam is attending the demonstration with a hand grenade in his pocket. its presence (like a rocket in his pocket) indicates what he is capable of doing.

but he is such a dreamer, this samuel melville. while the chants and slogans rise and fade, sam becomes eager. if only for a second, he wants to hear again the sonance of indian summer. the sound of heat rushing like a river in his ears.

and who should be driving up the crowded road, the sidewalks crowded by the police and demonstrators alike? who is honking his horn and making a nuisance of himself? why, it is death in his convertible.

. . . i've brought my girl friend, death announces with pride . . . her name is autumn . . . and i want you to meet her.

Chapter Nine

after meeting george demmerle at woodstock, sam melville returns to new york city. he doesn't see his new friend for several months. but sam doesn't waste time. he moves ahead with specific projects: he blows up the marine midland bank, and with other friends, he destroys the army headquarters in the federal building. sam and his friends are conducting a series of bombings through the autumn months. this form of sabotage is historical. but the name they give the process is new. they call it direct action. these activities are planned and discussed in meetings thick with polemics and cigarette smoke. the meetings are difficult and long. the american new left is developing its own vocabulary.

. . . c'mon, you people, sam complains . . . let's stop talking about theory, and get on with the work . . . i feel like we're jerking off with our mouths, you know?

. . . that's a sexist remark, sam.

. . . what the hell are you talking about? . . . what's so sexist about jerking off?

. . . i wish you would exercise more precise criticisms, sam.

. . . oh, yeah . . . just because i know what i want, you think i gotta talk about it all night long . . . that doesn't make any sense to me.

. . . and it doesn't make any sense for you to keep bringing up the name of george demmerle, sam . . . who is that guy, anyway?

sam melville decides to contact george demmerle in the month of november. his group is divided over a question of strategy. should they persist in sabotaging military plants related to america's war efforts? or should they refrain while nationally-planned peace marches are in effect?

. . . do you know who those marches are for? . . . they're for the weekend warriors who drive in from the suburbs to the big city . . . it makes them feel good to think they're doing something . . . they can even write a check to sponsor the next one . . . and while they march, the war goes on . . . it's a travesty . . . but i've got to do more than march in a parade. . . and if you don't want to hear that, i'm calling up george demmerle . . . george will know what to do.

it is a miserable night outside. the evening is cold and wet. dead leaves whirl-wind on the sidewalk. they scratch your face. this is a night to stay home and drink beer. the last person george demmerle expects to hear from when he answers the telephone is sam melville. he is shocked and delighted.

. . . yeah, george . . . i've got a plan . . . and i want you to be part of it.

george's face turns beet red. he flushes from the top of his head to the tip of his shoes. his luck is incredible. a one in a million shot has come true.

. . . why don't you come over to my apartment, and we can talk about it, george suggests.

after sam agrees, george hangs up the telephone without saying good-bye. he brays like a donkey . . . goddamn, he marvels . . . i've got the mad bomber right where i want him.

sam arrives at george's apartment late that night. after greeting george with an enthusiastic handshake, sam initiates a thorough search for surveillance devices. he unscrews the light sockets and the telephone receiver. he takes apart the shower head in the bathroom, and he runs his fingers through a box of wheaties in the kitchen. then he announces the place is clean, and, yes, let's sit down and talk, shall we?

george has trouble repressing a sneer. he walks into the kitchen muttering something about having another beer . . . jesus, what a guy, george shakes his head . . . but after i bust him, my salary is gonna increase tenfold . . . i'm gonna clock some big dollars, that's for sure.

he pulls out a thin reefer and lights it up . . . tell me about the plan, george asks. he sucks on the stick and then passes it to sam.

. . . we are going to demolish the army trucks parked by the national armory on lexington avenue and twenty-sixth street . . . i've got the dynamite . . . and it should be no problem, sam continues in earnest . . . because i've been doing this stuff for awhile.

hindsight is a cheap sensation. but let's consider the facts: george is a cop, and sam melville is proposing a felony crime. who do you think is going to win this contest? george's participation in the truck bombing is a test of his strength. it will determine whether or not he has a talent for guerrilla warfare. while he listens to the details of sam's proposal, george considers his own best interests. should he reach for his revolver and bust sam now? maybe he should be patient and let the situation develop. george puts two and two together: i've got to make sure this crazy fucker doesn't get me killed.

but to sam's face, george smiles. he puts out his hand for sam to shake, soul-brother style. it is one of the many tricks george has learned. his handshake is warm and firm. george has become a member of the woodstock nation, and he has never taken acid.

. . . sure, brother, he gulps . . . you can count me in.

when sam leaves george's apartment, a crowd splits in half down the middle of the street. two fifteen-year-old boys run into a pool of light. they stop and sniff the night air. they are alert to the spirit of danger. one of them removes a twenty-five caliber pistol from his windbreaker. the gun has a plated-steel barrel with a small and vicious muzzle. the boy draws his right arm, and when his hand is level with his chest, he fires a dozen shots into the crowd.

the girls and boys break away screaming. the girls' hairdos move in unison, like flags on display. everyone tries to run. the gunmen sprint into the park, and the crowd folds and divides. a girl faints. sam closes his eyes and takes a deep breath. he crosses his fingers. he hopes better days are ahead.

. . . these kids, george was saying to sam at woodstock . . . these kids don't know the pain, do they, sam?

. . . i'm as radical as anyone here, george boasts . . . but the kids, he laments . . . they don't trust me . . . they think i'm an old man.

sam spells out the core of george's problem: those who do not seize the historical impulse will be forgotten by it. how many times does he have to tell george? taking acid is the only method that can determine if he is cool.

. . . cool? george is perplexed . . . why do i have to be cool?

to be cool is everything, george. the world could fall apart, and it wouldn't matter. your cool would remain. it belongs to you and no one else. you are a fire on the mountain, impossible to reach. you are so down, the earthworms know your name. women love you because you last all night. you are the ice man, dig?

. . . think of it, sam . . . think of how it used to be . . . we got married and went to work . . . we came home to a wife who was dying in the living-room with hair curlers on her head . . . she had the look of a zombie in her eyes . . . and we were too tired to care.

george will never be cool. but he possesses valuable knowledge. he learned that friendships between men are based on definitions and plateaus of domination rather than mutual respect.

. . . you don't want to step outta line, george, the football coach said to him one day while playfully swatting him on the ass . . . because all of us thinking the same . . . that's what keeps the ball rolling. back at woodstock, women and men with sleeping bags tied around their shoulders stumble by george and sam. they are seeking nooks and crannies in the fields and groves to crash in. everyone is exercising the instinct of a mole burrowing for a warm and snug hole. the undercover cop turns to this target. the game of risk is about to begin.

i have found a vision of the underworld in george demmerle. twenty years have come and gone, but george remains on the job. he is addicted to information. in the meantime, he will settle for the names of your friends.
. . . i'll make a deal with you, he offers . . . i'll make sure you don't get hurt . . . you play with me, okay? . . . what do you say to that? he slaps me on the back.
he strikes a match and the darkness flares. his profile is a riot of distortion, elongated, stretched out and gray. without warning, he reaches out to stroke my neck. i am under the impression he is going to lean over and kiss me. george's laughter dies on his mouth and is buried in his eyes.
. . . i'll tell you what, he thumps me on the chest with the tip of his index finger . . . you provide me with news about sam melville . . . and i'll make sure the cops don't bother you.

why do the police fear the man? is it possible he will return from the dead? or can we say, when all is said and done, sam melville never died?
. . . my bosses told me the other day the melville case wasn't over, george admits, changing his tone . . . they say his status remains fugitive . . . you have the right to remain silent . . . you have the privilege of saying nothing . . . but any time you want to talk about it, you can call me at this number.
george demmerle drops a business card into my lap. he peers at me. his face is bathing in moonlight . . . come clean with me . . . and you'll be let off the hook, he promises . . . but if you don't . . . you'll keep writing this story . . . you'll be

writing it until you are old and tired.

   history is a hard ladder to climb. all you ever do is slip and fall on its worn out rungs. i don't care if this story doesn't have a conclusion. the card george demmerle has left remains in my lap. the undercover cop's parting words are tattooed into my heart . . . the case of sam melville is not over until we drive his memory from the public eye, he said.
   i suppose a policeman knows best. however, my duties are different. the police want to kill a rebel. but i am an underground writer. the uncollected debts of history are waiting to be repaid in full. it is my task to keep sam melville alive.

Chapter Ten: In the Day of the White Sedan

paranoia: it is the food of madness. paranoia is the daughter to fear. when you are alone and in trouble, ready to kiss her glossed lips, try opening your eyes, and you will see she looks a lot like her old man. paranoia causes blisters on the brain. it induces tunnel vision for charred eyes. the only object that retains meaning for a man stricken by fear is the policeman's car.

sam melville is experiencing a loss of weight in october. sleeping has become a problem in november. the longer a night drags itself out, keeping the dawn away, the more paranoid sam becomes. nowadays, the nights seem to go on forever. sam spends a great deal of time pacing in the apartment. he occupies himself with tedious chores; he lifts heavy boxes and sweeps the floor. his telephone conversations tend towards the cryptic. if you didn't know him well, you wouldn't know who you were talking to, so guarded are his words.

downstairs, the streets are wicked. pedestrians fill the boulevards and avenues, hiding behind wool scarves and big hats with the brims pulled low against the wind and sleet. the throngs of people become unrecognizable to each other. they skirt puddles of rain water while drifting towards the steamed windows of downtown pubs. they will do anything to get some place serving warm drinks on a day like this.

sam is carrying a revolver in a shoulder holster. he is not

familiar with the weapon: he wouldn't call it a friend. but paranoia has its own logic, and so, sam has acquired a new tool to treat his condition. he has taken to wearing a polyester-blend sports jacket to conceal the gun. to his friends, the jacket is an omen. it makes them wonder about a man who used to dress for winter in a t-shirt.

how true it is. fear eats the soul. sam doesn't want to talk on the telephone anymore. he thinks the phone is tapped. the instrument which conveys our tidings of sorrow and joy has become poison ivy in his ear. pleasure has become scarce. to look out the kitchen window at the white sedan parked across the way stirs bedlam in his mind.
. . . christ . . . they finally caught on to me . . . i never thought it would happen . . . i mean, i've been so careful . . . but on the other hand, i'm not surprised . . . the cops know everything . . . they are everywhere.
the trajectory of sam's life is reaching a watershed. his activities are starting to produce consequences. he touches his revolver . . . i hope like hell i don't have to use this, he confesses . . . i'd probably shoot myself in the foot with it . . . and the cops would charge me with attempted murder.

in the days of november the weather changes from white to gray. the sky turns to steel and lowers itself to the top of the city's skyscrapers, blotting out the sun. it gives the women and men in the street a keen sense of foreboding. the sky is suffocation's damp cloth; it falls to the sidewalks and subways below, calling for the hibernation of men and machines. it is going to be a hard winter. that is why the streets are emptying faster than usual during the five o'clock rush hour.
two men are sitting in the front seat of the white sedan. they smoke cigarettes and talk in a low monotone. they are comfortable with their habits. they are used to being patient. it is something they do as a team, and it goes without saying, they volunteered for the melville assignment.

paranoia attracts recruits into her camp with fluid ease. the two plainclothes cops know sam is upstairs in his apartment. he is their magnet; they are waiting for him to make a move. maybe he will commit an act that will permit an arrest. but as the superintendent down at the special unit told them, the evidence against sam melville was vague at best.

. . . george demmerle is pipelining rumors back to the office, the chief says . . . he's telling us the suspect has already admitted to a number of bombings.

. . . yeah, but you know how demmerle is, the two agents chorused their disdain . . . why, he's a loud-mouthed nut . . . and you can never trust a snitch even when he's working for you.

. . . that's why you boys are volunteering to check out the melville story . . . we gotta find out if demmerle is talking straight or what, the chief concludes.

the plainclothes cops are getting paid to be paranoid. they earn a lot of money being scared and throwing fear into others. but the salaries they command extracts its own tax from their flesh: they find it impossible to sleep without thrashing.

. . . my wife said i called her a crook . . . and she told me i punched her in the arm, the first cop says while sipping on a milkshake through a straw.

the second cop thinks about his aching back. his lips and throat are parched and running thin like a spit of sand in a pond. his hands rest on the steering wheel. his left foot is idly kicking the brake pedal.

the first cop's eyes are glued to sam's living room window. the curtains seem to be moving. but after a minute, he realizes it is the wind. he lights up another cigarette and relaxes. the pressure in his collarbone eases. he feels less anxious.

. . . and i've got to say it, he blurts out loud, startling his partner . . . it's that sort of creepy feeling you get when you collide with a spider's web in the basement . . . your first reflex is to cringe . . . you hate those insects, don't you? . . . you want to hit something . . . and that's what i did this morning . . . i hit my fucking wife.

he keeps talking to himself, illustrating certain points by flourishing his cigarette in the dark . . . i tell the little woman that everything will be all right . . . but she doesn't believe me . . . she rolls over in the bed with her back to me . . . i think i hear her crying . . . but to tell you the truth, i'm too scared to find out . . . i just lay there on my side of the bed until she goes to the bathroom.

. . . shut the fuck up, the second cop snaps, popping his bubble gum . . . here comes the woman who lives with the suspect . . . what's her name? . . . uh, yeah, it's jane . . . yeah, right, jane, he confirms.

the back seat of the white sedan is piled up high with fast food wrappers, empty cigarette packs and two twelve-gauge shotguns. the front windshield is filthy. it is smeared with a patina of dead flies, leaves, and advertising brochures stuck under the wipers. pigeon shit covers the vinyl roof, and some neighborhood kid ripped off the shortwave radio antenna the other night. the plainclothes cops are unable to broadcast transmissions to the chief. they are alone on their mission. the windows are rolled up tight. it smells bad inside the sedan. the policemen are in the world of their own, and they know it.

. . . are you scared, fuck face? the first cop asks his partner.

. . . nah . . . why should i be scared? he smiles.

it is a smile that wilts everything around it. the skin and the eyes turn into ruin.

. . . and besides, he admits, shifting his bulk in the driver's seat . . . i got this job because i like being scared . . . fear holds us together . . . say, could you hand me that hamburger resting on the dashboard? . . . yeah, the one in the greasy wrapper.

they complain about george demmerle in rancorous terms. george is not viewed with respect by the regular officers in the department . . . this faggot has been on the payroll for three years, smoking pot and trying to get laid by hippie chicks . . . and all he can come up with is this guy sam melville . . . george says this is the character who's been doing all the bombings lately . . . who the fuck knows? they shrug.

   winter's flu: stomach cramps. a shrivelling of the scrotum. swallow your cough medicine and take a heating pad to bed. sirens are shredding the distance between downtown and the river. your fever is getting worse. when you fall asleep tonight, don't be surprised if you have bad dreams.
   . . . a child's hand is caught in the cookie jar at an inappropriate moment, and her hand is slapped . . . a large bug lands on a baby's crib and proceeds to crawl towards the infant's head while the mother hums a song under her breath mere inches away . . . you bend over to pick up a dollar bill you have found on the sidewalk . . . the dollar is alone and without an owner . . . you tuck the money into your pocket, grinning at your good fortune . . . but a voice rings out, a voice larger than you are tall . . . hey, you, put that money back where you found it!
   . . . one morning you woke up to find your pillow covered with hair . . . you stumbled to the shower, turned on the faucet . . . and the rest of your hair swirled down the drain . . . you stepped out of the shower and looked into the mirror: paranoia made you go bald.

   sam melville parts the curtains with a practiced touch, as if he played cops and gangsters all of his life. it is hard to believe he was a draftsman in a reputable architectural firm. but things change. nothing stands still, including the fear of a man. sam melville is poised in the living room window with a revolver in his hand. his eyes are clear, and his stance is steady . . . those bastards will never take me alive, he rages.
   but after an hour, he goes to bed. he drapes the blankets around jane's shoulders and tucks them under her chin. she is already asleep, and he strokes her hair. he runs his finger-tips

over her crown. he reassures himself that everything will turn out fine.

. . . don't you think so, baby? he asks jane.

she mumbles in her sleep. sam smothers a laugh, careful not to wake her up. he holds her in his arms and listens to the ebb and flow of her breathing. sam met jane fourteen months ago, but they have lived together for a hundred years during nineteen sixty-nine. the idea of so much time compressed into one year makes him nervous. he decides to get up and go to the window again. before he can leave the bed, stealthy and cat-like as he is, jane's hand snatches his . . . where are you going? she asks.

. . . i'm giving a look out the window, honey, sam replies, extracting his hand from her sleepy grasp.

. . . oh, sam . . . give it up, jane yawns . . . they'll still be here in the morning.

and with that, she turned over on her side, pulled the blankets over her head and fell back to sleep.

sam crouches by the window. he runs his hand over the window-sill. he brings his fingers to his nose and then he sneezes. nothing has changed since he looked out the window two hours ago. the white sedan is parked across the street. a cat meows downstairs. a trash-can cover is rattling in the wind. the neighbor's water pipes are gurgling upstairs. sam melville holds his breath until he sees pin points of light behind his eyes. his life is getting shorter by the second. a reckless grin fastens itself to his mouth by sheer nerve. it flashes with brilliance. sam melville is getting ready for a showdown.

in the days of the white sedan, the president of the united states admits he is ill. paranoia rules the land with an iron fist. infant mortality is increasing as doctors are able to document a rise in the incidence of babies who refuse to leave the womb. when the president throws an apoplectic fit on national television, newspaper headlines wax archly: is armageddon around the corner?

the president's rouged lips and dyed hair were captured in lurid colors. television cameras focussed on the speeding ambulance that was coming to take him away. a crew of clean-cut men in white coats strapped him into a gurney. the president resembled a mummy with his teeth removed. he was in a state of shock. an intravenous tube dripped glucose into his naked arm. the tired vein with a needle puncturing the translucent skin; it was an image the nation would never forget.

a few days ago, sam melville told george demmerle about his connections to a national guerrilla organization. george is ecstatic. sam's words can be translated into silver and gold. george's brain reels from dreams of a snitch's paradise: cold cash in his pockets. in a burst of uninhibited name calling, sam divulges to george the places he has bombed: the united fruit company, the whitehall draft induction center, and the marine midland bank.

george listens to sam. he absorbs sam's narrative with the rapt attention of a child hearing a beautiful fairy tale for the first time. his eyes are glazed. he become euphoric as sam lists addresses and dates. he closes his eyes and imagines a shower of one-hundred dollar bills pouring out of the sky. a disembodied voice speaks to him, booming with majestic strength . . . this is god, george . . . and all of this money is for you.

later that night, george calls the offices of the federal bureau of investigation . . . i'm doing real good, he gloats . . . i've got the goods on sam melville . . . you wait and see.

a white sedan appears on the lower east side. it follows the trail over to sam and jane's apartment like a hunter after a deer. the police are taking george demmerle up on his information. they are gaining more interest in this man who calls himself sam melville.

meanwhile, the offices of general motors and chase

manhattan bank explode into charnel, ashes and smoke. each bomb damages another tower of babel, but falls short of destroying the building. legal papers, electric typewriters, desks, and chairs disintegrate, splintering. papers twirl in the chill november night, pulled along by gusts of unfriendly wind. glass covers the sidewalks (windows absolutely shattered and blown to bits). the police cordon off the area with yellow ticker tape. they begin to sift through the evidence. the investigation is inaugurated by flashlights in the deepest hours of the night. the newspaper will rant and rave over the story . . . bombs strike the city . . . the war has come home.

. . . do you see what i'm talking about! george demmerle yells into a pay-phone receiver . . . you people haven't paid me to inform for nothing! he brags . . . i'm gonna bring in sam melville.

this is a stage of reckoning before the end. the question is freedom. the answer is the same. but now we must wait. sam by his window-sill. the cops in their white sedan. george in the telephone booth . . . the snitch is hee-hawing into the receiver . . . his talking never ceases . . .

Chapter Eleven

on the afternoon of november the twelfth, sam melville meets george demmerle at three o'clock. they meet on a crowded street. they walk towards each other, heads bobbing and weaving through a chokehold of pedestrian traffic. the air is crisp, the day has turned out pleasant. every window shopper on the avenue is wearing a bright item of clothing. it's that kind of day.

. . . hey, brother . . . sam greets george by slapping him on the back.

george winces under the impact of sam's affectionate blow. his teeth snap together, sending a shooting pain down his jaw and then up into his brain where it registers like a red flag.

. . . cut it out, will ya? george complains.

mere hours before his supreme test, george is feeling unsure of himself, and all the more so, because sam melville reeks of good humor and cheer. sam may go up and down a staircase of emotions with manic haste, but when it comes to action, his intensity is a saving grace.

. . . this guy is gonna fuck me up somehow, george worries. the sidewalk blurs in front of his eyes. the noise of the street runs in his veins like ice water . . . he's some kind of nut . . . and something weird is gonna happen, i just know it.

. . . it's looking good, george, sam whispers, as they turn the corner onto a side street off houston. sam guides george by the elbow . . . we got one bomb already in position and ready to go off at . . . he consults his wrist watch. he is struggling to be patient. everything takes so damn long, it hurts . . . yeah, he says . . . the device will go off in exactly six hours.

sam realizes george is nervous. he discovers a tremor in the other man's eyes. george's lips are chapped, and he persists in flicking his tongue over them. george's tongue darts in between chipped teeth, trying to hide.
. . . you look kind of pale, george, sam probes . . . you're not thinking about copping out, are you?
george demmerle selects one of the many masks he can choose from when situations like this become difficult. it is part of his job. george is smooth enough: he knows how to fake a mood. but right now, george is scared . . . the fucking bastard, he whines . . . he's playing with my mind.
but for sam's sake, george strikes a fierce pose. his nose turns red. he closes his eyes and counts off the seconds . . . one . . . two . . . three . . . and then he thrusts his chin into sam melville's face, ranting . . . what are you accusing me of, huh? . . . are you trying to tell me i'm a coward or what? . . . if you feel that way about me, i don't know what you're doing.
. . . aw, relax, george, sam chuckles (he is mollified by george's piety) . . . i'm checking you out, that's all. the policeman permits a surge of self pity to play across his face. it is a visage bloated by too many drinks from the night before.
he had a bunch of money in his wallet with nothing to do. that's why he stayed at the bar until closing time. he tossed back nine bourbons in three hours of solitary drinking. he tried to win the bartender's attention, but she wouldn't have anything to do with him. he leered at the woman's legs. they were encased in canary-blue toreador pants.
. . . you sure are a nice lady, george flirted . . . and you have a big booty . . . do you mind if i touch it, nice and light?
. . . thanks, buddy . . . but i've got a boyfriend . . . and he doesn't say stuff like that to me . . . so why don't you be a good boy and go home and sleep it off.
george staggered home in the final hour before dawn. he left the bar in a noisy departure that required the bouncer's assistance. he couldn't find a taxi cab anywhere: he walked

fifty blocks alone. he talked to himself like a baby. he urinated on a garbage can outside his front door. the piss glowed under the street lights. it dribbled on his pants because he wasn't aiming. george fumbled with his keys and opened the door to his room . . . tomorrow is a big day, george demmerle said to an empty bed . . . i'm gonna bust sam melville . . . it's gonna make me a rich man.

quietude is the forgotten room in a big city. the absence of sound is a sign of impending trouble. we are approaching the zero hour. george demmerle pauses to squint at sam melville near the corner of first and houston. the wind has picked up velocity; it sends trash flying in the air. george shivers and wishes he had an aspirin. he zips up his windbreaker while sam unbuttons his shirt.
. . . shit, don't worry about me, george smirks . . . i'm sort of hung over . . . you know how it goes.
george hopes the contortion of his lips will pass for a smile. his mouth is tight and small . . . i can't blow my cover now, he reminds himself.
. . . now you're talking, georgie boy! sam chortles, flinging a brawny arm around george's hunched shoulders.
. . . don't call me georgie!
. . . what? . . . oh, okay . . . all right . . . here is what we are gonna do . . . you go home and change into clothes that have large pockets . . . you hear what i'm saying, george? . . . i want big pockets . . . c'mon, man, you can do it . . . and then you meet me at the second street apartment at eight o'clock . . . and we'll set the bombs.
the two men shake hands and say good-bye at the mouth of the subway. sam watches george recede into the black hole of public transportation, pushing and shoving his way to the token booth. while purchasing a token, george drops a handful of change to the pavement. he falls to his hands and knees to find the money.
. . . that george sure is nervous . . . but i don't hold it against him, sam says . . . this is his first big strike at the enemy.

if sam only knew the accuracy of his prediction. but irony will dictate a pointed reversal: george hasn't been able to turn over a major arrest. his record was looking bad until he met sam melville.

when darkness throws down the sun, jane unlocks the door, and the first thing she sees is the silhouette of sam melville crouching at the living room window. the apartment is pitch black. the street light hurls itself against sam's head, illuminating the hard lines of his face. it catches the moment in his eyes, the fear of the other world, the police down there . . .
. . . hush, he cautions her with one hand raised . . . they're back.
jane tiptoes over to the window. she sneaks a glance into the rain-spattered street. the sounds of distant cars rumble in her ears. the sidewalks are glittering from the sudden outpouring of moisture.
. . . oh my god, i thought they went away. she covers her mouth with a hand. the men in the white sedan have returned.

this is the onset of something that can't be described. jane recognizes the presence of trouble. she draws back, pressing herself against a wall farthest from the window. she is not only frightened but also overwhelmed by certainty. sometimes, the two emotions feel the same.
. . . don't go out tonight, sam, she pleads . . . something is going to go wrong.
sam takes jane's hand, and without thinking, he moves closer to her, allowing himself to stand in front of the window where the police can see him. tonight is cruel. rats run along the curb by the sewer. a harsh wind drives in from the river, ripping the stuffing out of a newspaper bin.
this is the crossroads where we meet. everyone makes a choice in this world. you can move to the sound of one song or another. accelerating historical forces have sam in their

clutches now. if sam could stop and lay down the burden of his generation, he would see his courage is the longing for a beautiful death.

. . . i've got to do it, jane, sam melville says, releasing her hand . . . i've got to go meet george.

let us say the words of supplication for sam melville and the millions of americans like him. let us not forget: we are alone, together in the darkness . . . crouching in the darkness . . .

after twilight, sam melville walks out the door to meet george demmerle. it is a journey of a thousand confusions. his tongue is coated with a metallic tasting sheen that inspires convulsive swallowing. each time he swallows, his stomach clenches, increasing the weight on his bowels. he strides through the streets with his head bent forward. beads of sweat are breaking out on his brow.

abandoned buildings yawn at him, and an occasional dog crosses his path, sniffing at his leg. he unbuckles his belt and feels better . . . until he hears the screech of car tires coming his way. but the noise is not his affair; the car passes him, and sam continues on his journey.

at the second street apartment, george watches sam prepare the dynamite and fuses by wiring them together with a timer. the lights in the apartment are dim. a ceramic living room lamp sitting on the coffee table sheds its rays on sam. he is kneeling in front of the coffee table and with his mouth tightly set, he works the fuses into the sticks, tying them together with a timer.

. . . the dynamite works well, sam indicates with a shrug . . . because it detonates cleanly, and it's not volatile . . . we don't have to worry about its transportation . . . this is how it's done, george, sam explains.

he holds up his handicraft for the undercover cop to see.

. . . this is how it's done, george mimics sam in silence. he wonders why his heart is beating so hard. it must be his nerves. george yearns for a valium, but he's too scared to ask sam for one.

sam places the bomb in a shoe box. it seems appropriate somehow. he looks up at george. his forehead is creased from concentration. he rubs his eyes, and they begin to water . . . i don't know why i'm doing this, he says . . . it's like i'm in a slow motion movie . . . am i doing this for real? . . . or am i watching myself do it? . . . i just don't get it . . . sometimes, i get so tired . . . anyway, jane told me i shouldn't go out tonight.

. . . who's jane? george asks.

sam stares at george. he purses his lips in disgust . . . what's the matter, george, are you losing it again? . . . you know who jane is . . . damn . . . you are so weird . . . ah, fuck it . . . let's stow the gab and get outta here.

the two conspirators parted company at second avenue and seventh street. sam was tugging on george's coat sleeve. he blessed the snitch with last minute instructions.

. . . you go one way, george, and i'll go the other . . . it's just in case we're being followed, okay?

george demmerle tries not to betray his emotions . . . poor fool, he thinks . . . he doesn't know the area is swarming with cops.

sam gets off the subway and gallops up the stairs to the street. he walks over to the army trucks whistling a tune and acting nonchalant. an i-don't-care attitude is written across his face. but what he sees cuts short the song in his mouth . . . shit, that's odd, he sputters.

the army trucks are parked on the north side of the street. they are situated by a quadrant of apartment buildings. sam's prior reconnaissance of his target had disclosed the opposite: the army trucks were parked far away from the apartments. at one time, they had been in a position where he could have destroyed them without harming anyone.

. . . i didn't expect this at all, he snorts, and he spins around angrily on his heel, stalking off towards twenty-fifth street to rendezvous with george.

george demmerle is stomping his feet in an effort to stay warm. a cigarette is cupped in his hand, and once in a while, he brings it to his lips, sipping on the butt as if smoke were liquid. he hawks a jet of phlegm to the pavement and wipes his nose with the back of his hand. he repeats and conforms the gesture. he is full of anxiety.

the police chief has ordered george to remain visible at the intersection until he is commanded to do otherwise. there are twenty special agents in the vicinity. they are waiting for sam melville by using george demmerle as the bait.

. . . but what about my protection, george wailed. he slumped over the chief's desk and wept. it was the night before the arrest. a senior lieutenant stood behind the chief's chair, lighting his pipe for him. he giggled and said . . . don't worry, snitch . . . we'll have twenty guns trained on you.

george takes another drag from his cigarette. his exposed back feels like a target in a pistol-shooting range. he hears footsteps approaching. oh, god, here he comes. he throws away the cigarette, committing himself to the act with violence: he flings the cigarette to the ground. this is the signal george demmerle has agreed to give the police when he sees sam melville at the intersection.

sam's pale face emerges from the shadows. his eyes are luminous among the faint colors of the street. george can see he is upset. sam's mouth is pinched and remote (it is a dying flower offered to a sacrifice).

. . . uh oh, george groans, he knows something is wrong.

the squadron of special agents see the cigarette flaming out on the sidewalk in a spray of short-lived embers. they move in, tightening the noose and smelling blood . . . hold your fire until i order you to shoot, one cops yells to another over a walkie-talkie. sam is paralyzed in mid-stride; his foot will never land on the pavement.

. . . hey, george, sam laughs bitterly . . . there seems to be a change in the plans without anyone telling me.

the hair on george demmerle's head bristles. he knows the weapons of the police are trained on a spot between his eyes. he can hear the bullets singing through the air. he attempts to calm himself by thinking about the reward money. he stands there. time is a jack-in-the-box waiting to spring with lethal intent.

. . . listen, george, sam melville grabs him by the arm . . . i'm going down the street . . . but i'll be right back, okay?

. . . take as long as you want to, sam, george stutters, shaking like a winter leaf.

the arrest begins behind your back, or it comes at you from the wings. a flash of metal from the corner of the eye. a rustling of the cloth. a creak of gun leather: you become catatonic in the presence of these elements.

. . . don't move, asshole, or i'll blow your fuckin' brains out! a cop screams.

he levels his service revolver at sam's head. sam's right hand is frozen at his chest. his left hand grips a duffel bag. the fingers are possessive and reluctant to let go. the shoe box bomb is ticking away safe and sound.

. . . drop it, man! another cop yells.

five more special agents surround sam. more police charge into the intersection bearing automatic assault rifles like spears. they are whooping and hollering. squad cars and police vans whip up to the curb, laying rubber in ear-splitting blasts. red, blue, and yellow beams are rotating, blinding everybody with refracted light.

. . . shoot the motherfucker!

. . . okay, you got me, sam gasps.

. . . don't move, melville.

. . . put the cuffs on him, damn it!

the first cop grabs him, yanking at the buttons on his jacket. the handcuffs bite into his wrists. the sharp steel cuts the flesh.

as soon as he hears the click of the lock, it becomes a sound he will never forget. the handcuff's click is a one-note melody (it's heard throughout the world), and it echoes in his ears for hours. he strains against the cops, pushing his heels into the pavement. nothing like this will ever happen again, he promises himself. he grunts when a cop punches him in the stomach. but he doesn't feel anything. in the middle of this, he smells the rain. the wind has died in the long night of a captured man.

. . take it easy, big boy, a beer-stinking voice barks in his face . . . take it easy . . . and you won't get hurt.

Chapter Twelve: The Interrogation

    his hands lay flat on the concrete wall. the surface of it grates against his face. he doesn't dare to breathe. an unknown number of policemen trample on his feet. sam is the center of attention.
    . . . don't move dirt bag, a cop spits . . . or i'll fuck you up but good.
    the ice cold barrel of a gun jabs him in the jugular vein, making it difficult to think or swallow. one heavy set cop bawls out the general orders while the other special agents scream at the top of their lungs. sam finds it hard to believe, given the weakness of his position, but he realizes the police are afraid of him. the cops are jumping up and down. they clobber each other while yelling war cries. they are going crazy because sam was armed. he had equalized the situation, and the police never like those odds.

    . . . remember, men, special agent hodgens said to his subordinates at the last meeting before the stake out . . . these people are simply evil . . . thieves and murderers . . . you know what sam melville is like . . . we see his counterparts on the evening news every night, don't we? . . . he is from the kingdom of violent niggers and white trash . . . he is an underclass stuntman with a gun.
    special agent hodgens resembles a novice priest conducting his first mass in a small town called nowhere. his earnest words and somber face clash with his untied shoes and worn

out suit. his voice is bordering on hysterical. but the men have heard it all before. some fidget but most of the agents absorb hodgens' words with an air of professional boredom.

. . . put your hands behind your back, melville! . . . do it, goddamn it! the cop shouts.

sam's arms are wrenched into a position that enables his shoulder sockets to perform the impossible. he thinks the handcuffs are too tight but he remains stoic; he doesn't say a thing.

. . . hah? . . . what did you say, asshole? the cop spins him around, and slaps sam on the jaw, almost knocking him down . . . did you say something about the handcuffs? . . . did you?

the policeman's visage is mottled and red. his head is bisected by a white riot squad helmet. he is six inches shorter than his captive; the stream of invectives he hurls at sam end up landing on the prisoner's chest. his words are punctuated by spittle. sam closes his eyes and listens to the noise.

there is something to an arrest when it is conducted at night that speaks to time without an end: the ride uptown in the back of an unmarked squad car seems to go on forever. the city lights blink as you drive by. but you are not part of them anymore. they glitter at you and say good-bye.

we have arrived at eternity: it is a room devoid of windows. fluorescent lights shine upon three chairs flung together. a metal table is bolted to the floor. an air conditioner rattles through the walls from another room. the interrogation is ready to begin.

the door opens and three men walk into the room. two of the men are cops and the third party is sam. before he is invited to sit down, sam is ordered to remove his clothes. this is the first step in describing the balance of power between a prisoner and the state. when one man is naked and the other carries a gun, we understand who has the upper hand. naked power is the truth. it is the first lesson we learned in school after we pledged our allegiance to the flag.

. . . okay, melville, one of the cops says poker-faced . . . you take off your pants and bend over.

sam attempts to comply with the request in a dignified manner. but this policy wears thin when he spies one of the cops pulling on a latex glove. once done, the policeman rests his left hand on sam's back and inserts a gloved finger into his rectum. the prisoner flinches. the cop digs his shoes into the floor, standing his ground, so to speak, to investigate a little further.

. . . nothing here . . . he's clean, the cop declares. he removes his finger from sam's colon. it comes out with a soft pop. the agent peels off the glove and drops it into a wastepaper basket. the kind that has a foot pedal to open and close the lid.

. . . you can stand up now, sam, special agent hodgens says. his perfectly parted hair looks like an expensive wig attached to an otherwise cheap and rumpled face. the agent glances at sam and snickers.

. . . put your clothes on, melville and let's talk.

guilt and fiction. it all comes together in a policeman's mouth. it is the story of wild deceit and frustrated lust. the grotesque and the implied. fiction is deadly enough to turn facts into lies. take a plunge beyond the surface and you will find the bottom.

. . . do you want a cup of coffee, sam?

sam melville watches the door open and close. another special agent has entered the room. he is young, and with complete disregard for the frozen stares of his colleagues, he smiles at sam.

. . . sam . . . my name is tom . . . and i'd like to ask you a few questions, if you don't mind . . . do you still want that cup of coffee? . . . sam? . . . sam?

. . . yeah, i'd like that, sam melville replies . . . that and a glass of water, please.

tom sinks into a chair across the table from sam. he hitches his belt and smiles again, displaying a row of capped teeth.

. . . well, sam, he begins . . . let's see now . . . united fruit company . . . marine midland bank . . . milwaukee . . . canada . . . you sure had us jumping for a while . . . you know that, don't you, sam?

the nice and easy college-educated smile disappears and a scowl takes its place. the room is quiet, save for the shuffling of someone's feet. it is late at night, and under the fluorescent lighting, each man looks green and seven years older than he is. sam coughs for a spell, and then he stifles the hacking by pinching his nose with his hand. the coughing went on and lingered. it made the cops chuckle.

. . . you know that guy is gonna die, tom says with a casual inflection of his youthful voice. but he acts like the words have been on his mind all night long.

. . . what guy? sam whispers.

. . . oh, you know . . . that guy over at the criminal courts building, tom ventures while studying the crease in his slacks. he uncrosses his legs and leaves the chair. he walks around the table until he is standing behind the prisoner.

. . . you mean the bomb went off? sam cannot hide his delight. the other cops sour when they notice his obvious pleasure. they begin to grumble.

. . . yeah, that's right, sam . . . and you'd better think about it, tom suggests (he stares at the bald spot on sam's head) . . . because that guy may lose his arm.

. . . you're lying to me, the prisoner says . . . there wasn't anyone in that building.

these are dangerous times. if you want to challenge the powers that be, you may lose or win. but the police will always have more guns. and the police have extra insurance to promote their victory. they possess a secret weapon in their arsenal. his name is george demmerle.

. . . where's george? sam melville demands . . . where's my brother?

the three policemen do not bother to answer his question. they sit in their chairs or stand; three sphinxes from police gazette hell. silence crashes over sam's head. he tears his eyes away from the triangle of cops surrounding him. he wants to escape the knowledge that remains unspoken in the room. but the truth dangles like a corpse from the scaffold. the cops won't say it; they never do, and so, sam melville will have to figure it out for himself. a picture of george's face, the well-fed cheeks and the stringy hair, the nicotine-stained fingers, all of this takes the stage in sam's mind. his eyes begin to sting.

. . . jesus christ . . . george squealed on me, sam melville trembles . . . my god, george demmerle was a fucking cop! he says with awe.

there are relationships which exist between adult males in america that evoke prehistory: it is impossible to forget the bondage of puberty and the ensuing fratricide in the locker-room. those moments enshrine the rites of the bully and the swine. the poor boy and the emerging drag queen.

boys will be boys. the world was changing through an examination of each other's bodies. george broke under the scrutiny. he shattered like glass. he didn't have a girlfriend and he didn't dress cool. george demmerle was a pariah. he became a locker-room snitch for the sake of vengeance.

. . . he stands alone in a junior high school gymnasium shower stall. naked, he is besieged by other naked boys. they taunt him while a nozzle shoots jets of scalding hot water onto his back. the boys whip his legs with wet towels that have been drenched in water and knotted in the right places for the job . . . hit the snitch! . . . hit the snitch!

the cry was electrifying. everyone lined up in the shower stall under jets of water to take their turn. even those boys who were ready to proceed on to the next class came back for a whack at george.

red welts streaked his arms and buttocks. he slipped and fell to his side. his collapse was accompanied by raucous cheering from the other boys. george was laying there in a miserable heap, sobbing and resting his injured ribs against the shower tile. the third period gym teacher walked into the shower stall. his high top sneakers were smacking with each step he took on the wet floor. he picked up a wet towel, sniffed at it gingerly, and then he glared at george.

. . . what's going on here? . . . huh? . . . what are you sitting there for, demmerle? . . . are you some kind of fucking queer? . . . put your clothes on and get outta here! the coach roared.

on his way to lunch that same day, george is accosted in the hallway by a familiar face. he groans and tries to squeeze through the crowd. he wants to flee but fails.
. . . where do you think you're going, georgie boy? hah? buddy grossman grabs him by the neck. he ruins george's paisley shirt in a single motion . . . you shouldn't have ratfinked on me, georgie . . . because now i have major problems . . . i'm gonna get expelled from school on account of you . . . and it's no fuckin' good . . . how are you gonna make it up to me, fat boy? . . . how are you gonna make the pain go away?
. . . i don't know! . . . i don't know! . . . george shrieks. he pulls himself free of buddy grossman, tearing his shirt into ribbons. he is desperate to lose himself in the crowd. but the crowd rebuffs him.
. . . that's the guy . . . he's the snitch . . . a ratfink . . . he dresses like a geek.
. . . i'm gonna kick the crap out of you with the tips of my pointed boots, buddy grossman announces for all to hear . . . i choose you off, he taps george on the nose . . . you'd better be in the alley behind mcdonald's at three o'clock.
. . . wow, everybody in the hallway mob shuddered. the tension ran among the crowd, setting the kids on fire with the news: buddy grossman is going to fight george demmerle after school.

george demmerle found his place in the american sun. he learned to counterfeit an image and sell it. he learned to bother tiny babies in their carriages when their mothers were not looking. hearing the babies cry makes george gleeful. but turning in left-wing radical bombers makes george important.
working for the police as a snitch is not easy. think of the

difficulty. george wears two separate identities, one on top of the other. he has spent a lot of time attending rock shows and night-clubs cultivating his persona. he tries hard to be seen in the chic eating and drinking spots of the city.

but he is the flotsam in a police department system. he lives in a hotel and he eats fast food. nobody ever asks him over for a couple of beers.

. . . how can we? the detectives down at the station ask . . . nobody likes a snitch . . . and besides . . . he shouldn't fraternize with us because that would expose his cover and his career would end . . . he'll lose his job.

the story doesn't end there. the only human being who likes george demmerle is sam melville. the underground bomber feels empathy for anyone who suffers.

the sensation of friendship has overwhelmed george. twin engines of love and hate channel through his brain. the two motors are seeking a common point of convergence that will never occur. when he is not busy hating sam, george demmerle almost forgets his job is to betray the man.

. . . this guy sam melville is the only revolutionary who isn't trying to force acid down my throat . . . and for that i am grateful, george demmerle continues to write in his report to the police chief. he is working feverishly with a pen and paper deep into the night.

. . . sam?
. . . wake up, sam.

sam melville is nodding off. the interrogation is arriving at a conclusion. special agent hodgens is combing his hair. he inspects himself in a hand-sized pocket mirror. he is satisfied with the view.

. . . by the way, sam . . . you know that fellow is going to die from the criminal courts bombing on center street, don't you?

the prisoner does not like what he is hearing. he isn't sure if hodgens is telling the truth. but he can't afford to doubt him either. earlier in the evening, the police let him know jane had been arrested at their fourth street apartment. the information drives sam to despair.

. . . oh, man . . . oh, man . . . she's just a kid . . . i can't let her take the rap on any of this, he thinks . . . they'll send her to the big house for seventy-five years.

. . . all right . . . i did it, sam melville confesses . . . i want to get it off my chest right now . . . are you guys ready for this?

special agent hodgens lays the pocket mirror on the table. he shifts his weight from one foot to the other. he lifts his pants to scratch a flea bite. he exposes a slender ankle above a drooping nylon sock.

. . . what i'm trying to say is that i did everything, sam tells him.

. . . did you make the phone calls, sam?

. . . yeah.

. . . did you write the communiques and deliver them to the news media yourself?

. . . that's right.

. . . did you plant the bombs, too?

. . . of course i did . . . i did it all, damn it! sam yells. he is losing his temper.

. . . then let's sign the form, sam . . . and we can get the hell outta here . . . i believe you could use some sleep if i'm not mistaken.

the agent removes a sheaf of documents from his jacket pocket. he brushes some invisible debris from his lapels and sneers at sam.

. . . what's that? sam asks. he smells disaster. the rotten carrot tied to the end of a stick.

the policeman grins. trickery and deception gladden his heart. it gives color to his haggard cheeks and lends the ring of authority to his voice . . . it's a statement of confession, melville, the special agent says . . . it's what we need you to sign if any of us are gonna leave this room tonight.

. . . forget it, sam melville snarls, the resentment rising from his throat, bored, tired and angry . . . i'm not signing anything until i see a lawyer.

Chapter Thirteen

a cold january day. squirrels hang upside down from the limbs of trees. icicles grow like fingernails from window-sills, growing longer with the night. someone has built a seven-foot snowman on the federal building's front steps. the snowman has acquired two red shotgun shells for eyes, and he possesses a wicked smile made from a tin can. the snowman retains his poise all day long, never fearing a meltdown because the sun is gone. but later, the afternoon wind comes up from the bottomless night, nickering and baring its teeth at children coming home from school. the wind bends over milkmen, torturing their hands when they unload crates of yogurt and butter. it is not a beautiful day. winter is tugging its ship of death from behind.

sam slouches in a wooden chair. he is sitting there waiting for the end of his trial. his lawyer has advised him not be impatient: the proceedings could go on until late spring. the days pass. the federal courtroom where he sits is a vast marble-covered arena. maroon-colored velour drapes cover the windows from the ceiling to the floor. a dozen cops are milling around the rear of the chamber near its double doors, murmuring and pointing fingers. they execute subtle gestures with their hands to indicate their hatred of the defendant. he has tried to escape twice since being confined in their custody, and once, he nearly succeeded. the morning passes into the afternoon. the police are dressed in silver and black suits. their jack boots creak as they walk up and down the aisles of the courtroom.

at the other end of the chamber, the judge's podium rises above the witness stand and the prosecutor's table. no one is higher to the ceiling than the judge. he slips on his bifocals and pretends to read a legal brief. but then, when he thinks no one is watching, he pats a manicured hand against his balding pate and yawns. he struggles to stay awake while the defense prepares itself for his verdict.

the courtroom clock is turning slender arms from left to right. time moves from left to right. time is the question on sam's mind.

. . . well, bill, what do you say? sam asks his lawyer . . . can you give me a round number . . . something i can work with?

bill whips out a yellow pencil, places it between his lips, gnaws on it for a reflective moment. his eyes mist over, and then he jots down a column of numbers in a notebook pad. he compiles the figures and bites his lip.

. . . it adds up to three hundred and seventy years of federal prison time, sam . . . and that's not including the new york state charges.

sam leans back in the chair. he lets a wave of dizziness pass over him. a month goes by. the muted gossip of the cops in the back. the clanking of the stenographer's machine. the district attorney coughing into a monogrammed handkerchief. a lazy fly circles the judge's podium. sam is aware of his own beating heart.

this is the killing floor. it is an hour before sam's conviction. bill has already admitted to sam that his case is hopeless. the history books will beg the question of his lawyer's competency, and in turn, the lawyer will criticize his client.

. . . you blew it, sam . . . you blew it because you gave the police a voluntary confession . . . their evidence on you was sketchy at best . . . christ, it was your word against george demmerle's.

. . . i had to protect jane and the others, sam explains in self-defence.

. . . what difference did that make, sam? his lawyer scoffs . . . they got busted, anyway . . . and because of your confession, the judge won't grant you bail . . . you're stuck in jail, man.

. . . what a goddamn ugly game this is, sam melville complains.

. . . shut up, sam, bill snaps . . . i'm doing the best i can.

every object in the courtroom reflects the hard light of fluorescence. the prosecutor's eyes, nose, and mouth give a spectator the distinct impression they were moulded from plastic. the federal marshalls' buttons shine with the brilliance of martial arrogance. sam discovers the judge is examining him over the rims of his glasses. his eyes are swimming from last night's hangover.

. . . are you prepared to speak on behalf of the defendant, mister crain?

. . . yes, your honor, the defense is ready to submit its plea.

. . . will the prosecuting attorney please join the defense's counsel in approaching the podium? the judge enunciates his request, droning, the weariness in his voice brimming over the courtroom like a waterfall.

(. . . you don't know how hard it is, the judge confided to his wife one evening in their kitchen . . . the idea of sending men off to prison for the rest of their natural lives is not an easy task . . . but somebody has got to do it, he says with a wry smile . . . and at least i am a fair and impartial judge of men.

he sips on the bourbon, enjoying its taste. the judge's wife opens her gown to show him her heavy breasts.

. . . oh, delilah, he laughs . . . do you want to have a fling in the hay with me? . . . is that it?)

bill rests his hand on the sleeve of sam melville's city prison uniform, but only for a second . . . are you ready to make that deal i told you about, sam?

a lawyer questions his client at the bridge to a crucial act. this is the station where lives are saved or broken through a procedure known as plea bargaining. it happens one hundred times a minute in courtrooms around the globe.

. . . trust me, the lawyer says . . . i am the butcher, and you are the meat . . . i shall spare the parts of you that i can . . . but the rest will have to be cut away . . . now get up there on the chopping block and do what i say.

sam rises to his feet. the carpeted floor greets his prison shoes.

. . . now walk fifteen paces and turn left at the bailiff's chair until you are standing in front of the judge's podium, sam . . . and then stand like a rock, champ, his lawyer advises . . . and don't worry . . . i'll be right behind you.

it is going to be the longest walk of sam melville's life. he glides across the courtroom floor holding his head high (he thinks pride will set him free. maybe he is right). he is unaware of the crowd gathering in the spectators' pews. quite a number of people have entered the courtroom to pay their respects to the captured man.

we know some of the people. but i prefer to think of them, and all the others i will never know as two hundred fifty million parts of you and myself. . . that's america . . . the faces of strangers and friends strain against a cordon of federal marshalls. the cops bellow and hit and kick to hold them back. the guards fear the throng will break through to the prisoner. sam walks alone in the center aisle towards the judge's podium where the prosecutor paces back and forth.

children crawl between the cops' legs and lay down a bed of flowers for the prisoner to step upon. each stride he takes to his prison sentence will be cushioned by gorgeous flowers. from the rear, an elderly man is wheelchaired into the courtroom by a male nurse. the old fellow seems to have been dug up from the grave. he is dishevelled in a pair of frayed pajamas that do not look clean.

. . . where's my son? he grumbles . . . where is that crazy boy?

. . . he's over here, sir . . . if i can get these people to move aside, i will bring you to him.

a great hush descends over the courtroom. a silence reminiscent of biblical movie settings from hollywood takes hold (with a string orchestra setting the mood; the crescendo peaking before the violin solo). sam melville's father has arrived to pay homage to his first-born son.

the nurse wheels sam's father up the aisle. the noise penetrates sam's veil, the protective coating he wraps around his brain so that he can endure the courtroom's proceedings. he turns around to witness the impossible.

. . . dad, . . . oh christ . . . i thought you were dead!

the old man pushes himself over to sam. his wheelchair is grinding under the flowers in the aisle. the judge is banging his gravel with such force, his glasses are jarred from his head. words ignite like a string of fire crackers in his mouth . . . i'm gonna call out the riot squad, the judge screeches.

. . . my son, sam's father takes his hand . . . i am dead, he croaks . . . but nothing would stop me from being with you today.

the riot squad burst into the courtroom equipped with tear-gas guns, and the crowd went crazy. the struggle for freedom does not stop at death. now is the time to speak, to take the chances you were never given. if you do not raise your voice, sam melville, your struggle will never climax.

. . . go ahead, sam, his father lays a ruined hand on his son's arm . . . everyone here wants to know why you did it . . . tell us sam . . . and don't be shy, his dad chides . . . tell us the truth.

. . . goddamn it, dad! . . . you know i can't explain my motivations, sam fumes . . . it's not an explanation . . . it's a dream . . . i have given my spare change to the lepers of the city on a platter of tin . . . i have seen the end of the world . . . my skin is pitted from too many nights spent alone . . . i am a man who wears broken shoes . . . one shoe does not resemble the other . . . i lost the desire to talk . . . and damn it, now my voice betrays me.

. . . i am the city's bootstrap . . . pull hard on me, and i will snap . . . but don't ask me questions, dad, because i can only tell you one thing . . . i was depressed.

sam melville's epitaph has its origins on a map of unreported incidents. the trajectory of his dissent can be measured by the buildings he chose to attack. each bomb he planted was an expression of his contempt for the government of this country. by nature, all measures taken against conformity are violent.

tears run down the eroded cheeks of the old man . . . you don't look so good, dad, sam frets, worrying his hands around the collar of his father's pajamas, making sure his scrawny neck is covered. father melville honks his nose into a roll of pink toilet paper.

the judge is tapping his gavel. the bailiffs are getting restless. the flowers are wilting on the floor. they die while exuding a comforting reminder of summer. time is running out for sam melville.
 . . . c'mon, sam, his lawyer tugs him by the elbow to the judge's podium.
 . . . what's the rush, bill, sam grins . . . i thought i had three hundred and seventy years on my hands.
 . . . i'm sorry, sam, but i have other clients, too, you know . . . and they need my services as well, bill retorts.
this is the hour when feet begin to drag. the sun has resolved to call it a day. the hands of the clock are slowing down, and eventually, they will come to a complete halt. people talk in the streets. the minutes pass. throats overflow

with questions . . . didja fuck her, huh?

on days like this, love is a faraway island. voices slip to the floor and dart away under the double doors. he has reached the end of the line. sam melville stands before the judge and the sentencing commences.

. . . you realize that even though you are pleading guilty to the crimes you are charged with . . . you are doing so because you know you are guilty . . . and not because you have been offered a reduced prison sentence, the judge thunders. he is oblivious to everything, but the roar of his own oration.

. . . yes, your honor . . . i know i am making a deal to reduce a three hundred and seventy year sentence down to a more tolerable eighteen years . . . i plead guilty to complete the deal . . . good bye, dad . . . say good-bye to jane for me.

let's make a deal. sam looks at bill. but his lawyer straightens his tie, consults his watch and acts distracted. sam has fulfilled his end of the bargain. but he can't believe this macabre drama of courtroom politics is happening to him. with his own tongue, he gave away his freedom. his lawyer told him there wasn't much choice.

. . . this is your best bet to get out of prison before you're an old man, sam.

the sun is going down (bright and fierce like a sunkist orange from hell). a new moon will appear in the city tonight. it is may of nineteen-seventy. the jets from the air force bases in california are flying to vietnam every eight minutes. they are carrying cargos of munitions and conscripted young men from alabama and the great midwest.

somehow it doesn't seem real. a madness has swept over the young nation (and this country will take a hundred years to die). college students are being murdered by the police. young blood is trickling in the gutters of our finest universities. sam melville hears the news on his way to a new york state prison. he is manacled to a seat in a bus with fifty other convicts. sam falls asleep in his seat to the rhythm of the bus and its shifting gears.

will we be able to stop the blood-drenched wheel before it rolls over us? everyone but the masters of this land is so damn tired. but maybe it is true. i once heard it said: those who do not falter before history are free to escape it. they will live again.

for the sake of sam melville and the other prisoners on the bus, i hope i have the strength to find out.

Chapter Fourteen: In the Land of a Thousand Push-Ups

these words are not a celebration of violence. on the contrary, they are a recognition of the need to speak in tongues. i talk for america. i am in a trance: the voices of strangers are planting their seeds into my mouth. i am a child of the atom bomb. destruction does not bother me because there is no tomorrow. but for sam melville in attica state prison, the situation is different. all languages flow to the same point: he must stand up and name himself, or lay down on the cold prison floor and die.

when sam completes his first one hundred push-ups, he gets to this feet, stretches his arms and rolls his neck. he springs like a cat to the cement floor and performs one hundred more push-ups. when he counts off five hundred repetitions, he flops over on his back, and without a discernible pause, he switches to sit-ups and repeats the process.

sweat drips from his brow. exercise has become a form of self-exploration. boredom can kill you, he says, but if you are smart, you can get past it by pushing your body into a state of transcendental awareness. sam melville is similar to many prisoners at attica state prison: he is able to execute one thousand push-ups a day. if the sensory deprivation of penitentiary conditions doesn't crush him, it is because discipline has saved him.

he is shadow boxing. he takes a right upper cut and then a left hook, sparring with the rough concrete walls, jabbing them left and right, dancing up and down on his toes because there is nowhere to go. the walls are so close, it is amazing he can breathe. it is a victory for a prisoner in the garden of misery.

. . . that night when i went out with george to blow up the army trucks on lexington avenue, i knew i was being followed . . . i knew the heat was coming down . . . but i had to prove myself . . . i couldn't give in to the fear and shame.

sam completes a set of deep knee-bends. his shoulders are level, and his eyes are half-closed, distant. he performs calisthenics as a prelude to yoga.

. . . i didn't understand my longing for death until i got to this place . . . now things are different . . . in prisons you have to learn to breath in tiny cells . . . and if i'm gonna think about george demmerle without freaking out, i've got to learn how to breathe all over again . . .

george demmerle is slumping over an open toilet seat. he is embracing the bowl with both arms. it seems he has a drinking problem. (he's a porcelain angel worshipping at the altar of piss.)

he is discovering the pleasures of the harbor: george is drinking the day away in a newark bar. considering the early hour, the tavern is vibrant with song and the festive spirit. the jukebox is blaring old forty-five records. the pool tables are occupied by the sound of billiard balls clicking and connecting with the velvet pockets. the cloying sweetness of marijuana smoke wafts from a booth in the back. it smells like columbian to me. when george returns from the bathroom, wiping his mouth, tucking in his shirt, and combing his hair, a middle-aged woman in a sequined gown asks him if he wants a date, or at least, would he buy her a drink.

. . . i'll do both, he says . . . by the way, my name is george . . . what's your name, little lady? . . . but first, you've got to tell me who does your hair . . . that frosted look is remarkable, my dear.

. . . my name is shirley, and marcello's on twenty-first

street, he does my hair . . . since you and i are getting friendly, george . . . how would you like a blow job using a rubber for fifty bucks?

george lights up a menthol cigarette and smiles . . . how about twenty-five dollars? . . . we'll call it bargain coming from the generosity of your heart and mouth, shirley.

. . . that's no way to treat a lady, george . . . and if you don't mind, i think i'll say good-bye.

shirley walks away without saying thank you for the drink (which she left untouched at the bar). george watches her saunter out the door into the bold sunlight. ungrateful bitch, he sniffs. he reaches for her drink, and without thinking, he tosses it back in a single gulp. he is going to get drunk, and while he is at it, he will smoke a pack of kools cigarettes in one sitting.

the afternoon vanishes into the bottom of a beer glass. while george's brain loosens up, the complexities about his job multiply. george demmerle considers himself part of a historical center. in his own blurred eyes (he sees them in the bar's mirror), george has become the hard core of law and order. he is the first string of our social fabric.

. . . i guard the borders . . . i saved america from sam melville . . . and i gave the country myself . . . i should have gotten a medal for his capture . . . but all i received was a lousy bonus which i drank up in six months going to the finest bars in the city.

the following day: it is a sweltering morning in the city. a shabby apartment takes its place among the others, revealing neither pride nor distinction. the street is not busy, and the front steps are empty. the heat is so unrelenting, no one is sitting on the stoop, enjoying its comforts. a dealer walks by with a gun in his hand. he holds his dick and searches for customers and friends who owe him money. a police car follows him. the cops are hot on the trail for contraband.

this is life after the cold war years: the age of scarcity has deposited george demmerle in a third-floor apartment where the ceiling is caving in.

the living room furniture appears to be suffering from the disease of rickets. the legs of the scattered chairs and tables are warped. layers of wall-paper bulge and recede. beer bottles are stacked up in a kitchen corner. rolls of toilet paper are unraveled in long trails over the furniture and floor.
george is sleeping on a fold-out bed when the telephone starts to ring. the bells sound off seven times, insisting upon his response. he dozes under a blue bed sheet. his shut eyelids are threaded with purple veins that travel to the bridge of his often broken nose. his cheeks bear the faded scars of razor burns. a radio sits on the kitchen counter, bleating out a song . . . give it up now, baby . . . give it up now . . .
the sleeping man surrenders himself to suggestions. war or peace. a new pair of pants. a kiss from a slightly famous movie actress . . . the telephone's bells persist in their clangor, and he stirs under the sheet, coughing and farting simultaneously.
he rises in anger to meet its irritating greeting. he lifts himself up from the sagging bed like a whale spouting water in the ocean. the blue sheet drops from his body. we are left with the image of a man who is tormented by eczema. red stripes cover his thighs, scaling and itching. layers of transparent skin flake from his stomach. he brushes them off with a weary hand. he coughs once more. the unexpected humidity of the day is filling his lungs with fluid. christ, who could it be? he wonders. dead silence greets him from the other end of the line.
. . . hello? . . . who's there? he rasps.

aching george. he afflicted with stool pigeon's fever. his temperature is running above normal, and he needs to take a bath. his gaze is dull; a flight of raw thoughts over an empty bowl. through the plastic tarpaulin that serves as his kitchen window, he looks up at the sky.

if a stool pigeon is deep within the throes of a fever, not only will his skin break out in unpleasant sores that open and ooze, he will also record gossip and rumors with zeal. he exhibits great care with the report's penmanship, unless he has access to a typewriter, and then, there is no end to a snitch's ravings. however, george demmerle is displaying dangerous symptoms, so extreme is his delirium: he keeps all the information in his head.

stool pigeon's fever is latent in most american children. our model youth has its price; most girls and boys are cheap and willing to perform. the illness tends to ripen and flourish during adolescence. the number of flare-ups (accompanied by blisters on the face and hands) increases dramatically after the age of twenty. the fever is known to linger throughout adulthood.

like most snitches, george is torn by the necessary and contradicting emotions of guilt and grandeur. in order to retain professional competency (and to earn his annual bonus), george has been forced to polarize his world view.

. . . i'm a bastard, a red-eyed george demmerle says over the first cup of coffee in the morning . . . i sent him to attica . . . it's the last stop in the penal system.

but later, george is prancing around the living room, holding the bed sheet to his chest and knocking over the lamps . . . he had it coming . . . i did what i had to . . . i am an official employee of the city's police department . . . it's my job to turn in criminals.

stool pigeon's fever is fatal. medical records show more americans are dying from politics than cancer every day.

the chief politico on the planet today has something to say. death walks a snitch's mile in george demmerle's shoes. death put his unwashed feet in george's unfashionable brown shoes.

. . . i want you to do me a favor, young man, death calls on

george . . . i want you to turn in someone who trusts you.
 . . . that's going to be hard, boss, george stutters . . . because no one likes me.
 . . listen, george, death warns . . . you have got to come up with a major killing . . . your own position is at stake here.

death scolds him while doffing his top hat to a young mother and her child out for a stroll in the sunshine, the morning dew.

 . . . you'd better get with it, george . . . i've got a million folks like you in every city . . . in my book, unless you prove yourself, you are one more number whose projected destination is infinity.

sam melville approaches one thousand push-ups. he is thinking about the moon and how far away it is. the moon is a ship that went to sea and never returned to gladden his eyes. sam melville hasn't seen the moon for two years.

his breath is regular, and his pulse is steady. he concentrates on controlling every fiber of his musculature, clenching and releasing the tendons in his arms and legs. the rush of blood into the canals behind his eyes almost blinds him. all objects in his line of vision dissipate into kaleidoscopic patterns. dot matrix hallucinations replace the prison walls.

he pushes harder. his face contorts into harsh ridges and folds. sweat cascades over his lips, dripping tears of pure water. he is an equation of flesh and blood pitted against a division of concrete and steel.

the mask is coming off. prison life helps him slough old skin. the new man is emerging. these are the days of reckoning. a snitch is troubled by a fever. but his victim will continue the journey of a thousand push-ups. little does sam melville know, but the eyes of america are upon him and the attica brothers.

Chapter Fifteen

the muscles on his back are something to see. dorsal fins ripple across an expanse of damp skin, churning and writhing to the rhythm of his lungs. he gulps a draught of fetid air, distending the veins of his neck until they stand out like the wires of a stolen car.

a headache is sending a knife into his temples. the headache is a signal: it slashes his throat and then it stabs his solar plexus, sending a message to the brain: i've got to get out of this place.

hallucinations sprout with relative ease in the fertile soil of the prisoner's mind. the need to escape is the flight toward desire. the prison talks to him during the night. guards open the tight slot to his door and whisper . . . melville . . . sam melville the mad bomber . . . he looks like a whipped dog to me . . .

they laugh and continue their watch, banging their truncheons on the steel doors. their batons tap out a tune of dread and loathing. their song pays respectful homage to their employer, the great man who sits on a throne of skulls.

. . . sure enough, that's me, death admits with conceit . . . i pay the wages to keep those guards healthy and alive.

sam melville. how he does it, we can't understand. cold sweating in the state penitentiary, the mind of the imprisoned man will stop at nothing to set itself free.

there is no entity more despised or envied than an escaped

prisoner. nobody else can embody the conflicts of this nation so clearly. a convict languishes in his cell inside every one of us. he is waiting to escape.

it seems like a dream come true when you hear the news on television. not only is everyone frightened, they are jealous, too. we give thanks or we cry. life is sweet when our prospects are in front of us. i like to think about the way things were and how they could be. i keep looking down the road, waiting for an escaped prisoner to appear.

. . . he is running across dusty brown hills. they are almost bald without grass or weeds. he skirts the wreckage of six farming machines. tractors and harvesters rusting in the sun, like dinosaurs from the days of old. a drought is casting a yellow glaze over the land, ancient and terrible in its strength of locusts and heat. sam melville is running towards the sun.

if the stones he stumbles over is the host (and the earth we trod upon), then the stone is the grandfather to all things. the sun is a child of grandfather stone. the sun is a relative to sam and all living beings. this is what the indians of new york would say.

. . . c'mon, sam, the sun urges him . . . get closer to me, and your problems will be over.

. . . are they behind me? sam pants . . . do you see those cops and their dogs coming to get me?

. . . i'll tell you what, sam, the sun replies . . . i gave you a powerful body to keep you going from the moment of your birth to the erasure of death . . . don't worry about those cops . . . they're nothing compared to you, boy, the sun guffaws.

. . . but how will i die? . . . you know they're not gonna let me out of prison without a fight . . . can you tell me that, huh?

sam trips over a pot-hole on a dirt road. the sun pouts. he retreats behind a bank of clouds coming over the border from canada . . . goddamn it, sam . . . i can't tell you that . . . it would be cheating.

this country is built around a fear of death. we are unable to discuss the future. but the sun relents, throwing rays over the drought-plagued fields of wyoming county. a billion locusts take flight. their chitinous bodies gleam imperial with the help of the sun.

. . . all right, sam, the voice of the sun softens. sam's eyes dilate to the sudden brilliance that pours on his face.

. . . it will be like this . . . you'll die two deaths . . . one death will be the official report the prison authorities release to the press . . . full of exaggerations and falsehoods . . . the other death? . . . well, that death will be yours alone . . . it's my gift to you . . . i made that promise on the day you were born.

sam halts in the road, choking in the dust while shielding his eyes. he scoops up a handful of dust and flings it at the fiery orb hanging low over the apple orchard, south of the village named batavia.

. . . thanks a lot, old man! he screams.

he sprints across an alfalfa field, zigzagging past rotting haystacks and barbed-wire fences. green snakes are sunning themselves on granite outcroppings. they hiss at him when he goes by. their forked tongues flicker like red candles.

the late summer heat parches the countryside. the land has been leached of water. the red clay lining the banks of dry creeks has turned into sun-baked brick. here and there, at the edge of a picket fence, a dead cow lays on its side. vermin bore a tunnel into the cow's eye sockets and nostrils. the vermin are on an expedition to the foodstuffs of the entrails.

the sun goes to sleep behind a mountain. when it wakes up again, feeling refreshed and adventurous, a curious notion crosses its mind . . . hmm, the sun broods . . . i wonder what sam melville is up to.

from his vantage point the sun can see the police are gaining on the escaped convict. he hopes sam will not end up in solitary confinement because of this caper. but he knows there isn't anything he can do to help.

sam does not know this, but the sun is sick. the sun knows

his cycle is coming to an end. he can sense the cancer spreading in his body. mutant cells are taking up habitation in his vital organs, corroding the need for food and drink. the doctors believe it is a generalized malaise.

. . . lymphatic cancer, the surgeons said after the initial examination . . . and that's just the start . . . this guy is really sick.

the sun laid behind the surgical screen and eavesdropped on their diagnosis even though he wasn't supposed to listen. he lolled on an operating table and suppressed the urge to hiccup, fearing he would blow out the hospital's windows if he dared to.

when he leaves the hospital, he reads in the newspapers that sam melville has been picked up by the police. there is a photograph of sam surrounded by a squadron of plainclothes agents. they are escorting him to a police van. sam does not have an expression on his face. it is safe to say, he seems remote when the light bulbs flash in his eyes. the photographs will stamp his image into an evening edition of the news. the man is becoming a star, the sun thinks.

the dusk falls over his shoulders like a dirty coat. he is a picture in black and white; no other colors could describe his condition as eloquently. his prison sallow skin is burned by the sun. his arms are cream white and tend towards a lighter shade of gray when he crosses into the shade. the collar and bib of his shirt are streaked with wisps of spiders' nests and flies' wings. twigs and burrs, feathers and leaves; the detritus of the countryside finds its way into his hair. sharp and dry smells from the soil, the acrid tang of animal deaths stings his nose.

rodents spy on him from their burrows, cowering in their holes, chittering madly when he looses his footing and slips to one knee. he catches a clump of grass in his fist, holding it, feeling the life within the slender shoots before he lets them go. he notices his shoelaces are untied, but he can't stop now: the insect buzz of a helicopter is drawing nearer.

he fears he is going insane, or worse, that he isn't going anywhere. but even more discouraging, when the wind shifts from north to south, he can hear the howling of police dogs.

a tango floats through his head. some kind of anthem from the downtown cocktail lounges of the nineteen-fifties. george would know the song and the band that played it, sam muses.

his torn shirt sleeves are flapping in the breeze. twilight shakes the land as if it were a hand. it squeezes the drought-stricken fields like fingers, crushing them until daylight disappears, leaving behind just some velvet darkness. he is dizzy, and he starts to speculate whether thirst and hunger will beat the police in claiming him as their prisoner.

a patch of neon over to the west announces the presence of a police roadblock. bats zoom around sam's head, squeaking as they try to bite him. the moon climbs the branches of a tree and bids him good evening. the night is too quiet. fire-flies extinguish themselves, and the crickets cease their chirping. an owl hoots once in warning and then a police helicopter tears into view . . .

he ducks for cover, contracting himself under a nettle bush, wishing he could disappear. but it is too late. sam melville is engulfed in a blazing halo of light. the helicopter's blades shear away his sense of balance, and he sprawls in the dust. the last thing he hears before he passes out is the crackle of the helicopter's loudspeaker . . . don't move, melville . . . and that's an order . . .

cold sweating in his cell at the break of dawn. he lays there on his bunk. his eyes are glued shut in a dream. one leg shakes. he emits a deep growl like a dog when it observes a minor threat to its safety.

what could it be? how do we compare the hunger for emancipation to an escape from reality? both windows lead to the same horizon: the prisoner is getting closer to the attica state prison rebellion. how many days will it be before he is set free?

Chapter Sixteen

the headaches. whenever sam melville refuses to stand at attention with his arms folded on the march to the cafeteria, he is placed in solitary confinement. he is escorted back to his cell and locked behind a solid steel door for twenty-four hours a day until the warden feels inclined to let him out.

you would think this high-strung man would twist and break (bolts of white lightning erupting from his skull). but defiance has its own rewards. keeplock affords him the privacy and quietude he cannot usually obtain in the overcrowded prison. if anything, the prison's noise, the accumulated venom and rage punctuated by an endless scream, this will kill sam melville and the other inmates before they are freed. noise is the enemy of any man who wants to think.

. . . all right, melville . . . fall out of formation and turn about face . . . do not look to either side until i tell you to run . . . but first i want you to fold your arms . . . what? . . . i don't care what your problem is, prisoner . . . you do as i say . . . take your hands outta your pockets.

the guard is tall and fat. dark shadows and mean lines occupy the corners of his mouth and the depths of his sunken eyes. he taps a polished club against his leg. he is waiting for sam to comply with his directive. the other men watch the confrontation between a guard and his prisoner. they are experiencing the calm before a storm.

sam exhales and tilts forward onto the balls of his feet. a memory emerges from his thoughts; he remembers the heroic statues in the museums of new york city. an unmovable feast of a man, he refuses to fold his arms. he raises his eyes from the penitentiary floor in a steady arc until he catches the guard with his gaze. the other prisoners standing in line are ambivalent: they could attack the guard or better yet, they won't get involved. without saying a word, they agree to a man, they will leave that decision up to sam. but other voices drift in the corridor from the adjacent tier.

. . . that's showing him . . . fuck the hacks . . . yo, eggbo . . . tin cups rattle against the cell bars up and down the main line. the cacophony is ragged. but then the cadence starts to grow, bringing on the noise.

. . . shut up! the guard erupts . . . or i'll get the warden to gas this wing!

the banging of tin cups fades out. it seems the battle is finished (with order maintained) . . . until a stiletto thin voice cuts in . . . and while you're at it, boyle . . . why don't you bring your mother down here . . . we'll turn her out front and back . . . just like we did your wife and kid brother . . .

the guard loses his composure in slow motion. his mouth sags and the whites of his eyes turn brown. the facial tic he saw the neurologist for, it winds up again like an alarm clock. boyle is separated from his wife. she went to stay with her family in albany seven weeks ago.

life is hell, he moans. he smashes his truncheon on the wall behind sam melville's head once, twice, three, four times, losing count when the club shatters, splintering into pieces. his face comes apart. it resembles a wet towel in a washing machine, wrinkled and raw . . . shut the fuck up! he howls . . . or i'll send everyone of you to the box!

. . . your mother sucks cocks in hell, boyle . . . the invective echoes in the corridor, caroming off the moist walls . . . sucks cocks in hell, boyle . . . boyle . . .

turn up the volume: these are the weeks before the attica

state prison uprising. the indian summer heat has become a nervous system killer. the heat cooks the brain through the months of july and august. september begins to percolate. you think your head is going to burst like a plastic bag filled with water . . . and it does.

it is a summer of bad food. gray-paste pork cubes are served two or three times a day. breakfast, lunch, and supper taste six months old by the time it reaches your mouth. you swallow each bite condemned to a pork-induced thirst.

every night after the lights go out, the screws make their rounds on the tiers. the scuffling of their boots muffles the rapping of their clubs against the cell bars. those clubs have beaten you black and blue on the parts of your body that aren't turning yellow.

boyle is considered a bully by the prisoners . . . he's a bad motherfucker who won't hesitate to use his bat on your balls and head . . . especially when he's got the other hacks with him . . . one to hold your legs and the other to pin your arms back while boyle works over your face . . . he's a bastard, the convicts declare.

but for some reason, he won't attack sam melville. his reluctance to use the badge of his office is rooted in the eccentricities of rural culture. consider this: boyle was raised in a village where cosmopolitan influences are regarded as decadent. in time, urban thinking was driven out of the small towns. superstition was allowed to flourish.

for the most part, this nation's mythology has died with the indians. but the provincial concepts brought over to the new world by the peasantry and the gentry of europe remain intact. a horror of the unknown is a fact of life for village inhabitants like boyle. the sight of sam melville's dead green eye fills him with terror.

. . . sam melville is trying to cast a hex on me with that evil eye of his, i am sure of this . . .

. . . c'mon, melville . . . let's go to your cell, boyle orders the prisoner. sam grins the smile of a juvenile delinquent who broke the school windows. everyone knows he committed the act. but no one can prove it.

. . . hey, boyle, he drawls . . . i think i got something in my eye . . . would you mind taking a look at it?

the hack keeps himself at arm's distance from sam melville. the prisoners check him out. they would enjoy beating on his corpulent body. where the hell are the other hacks? a siren goes off but no one shows up to rescue him. he hears footsteps running in a distant corridor.

. . . look at my eye, boyle . . . i need your opinion.

. . . i'm warning you, melville! boyle flinches. his face disintegrates into a thousand tiny facets, each one more fragmented than its predecessor.

sam faces a row of anonymous doors married to the cold and merciless floors and walls. he turns to face his tormentor. six hundred pairs of ears are trained upon them.

. . . did you say something, boyle? . . . something you might regret? . . . you realize, boyle, don't you? . . . that if you lay a finger on me . . . that finger will fall off by sundown?

. . . just get in the cage, melville, boyle says, his tongue a pile of ashes, the words having no strength in them . . . just get in your cell . . . and i won't report your behavior.

. . . that's good . . . that's real good, boyle . . . because now you're learning the code of a world to come . . .

in the days before the uprising, sam melville is taken from the main line and placed into segregation. his separation from the general population is the mirror of a paradox. sam's departure into solitary confinement is a reflection of his popularity among the brothers. he is considered a symbol of resistance among men who do not give their allegiance to anyone but their own kind.

. . . melville is a jew boy, right? . . . well, if he can gain the respect of the niggers and the spics, then we are in serious trouble, the lieutenant from the night shift said . . . we gotta deal this sam melville guy a bad card . . . we gotta keep him in the hole.

. . . hey, sam, when are you coming back?

the question fills the dank cages. it carries to the highest tier and then swoops down to the punishment cells below. behind every door is a convicted man. their eyes are comparable to the works of the christian renaissance painters. the colors are subdued. their intent is transferred to the viewer: who is the criminal? is it me or you?

the headaches visit sam in solitary confinement. they seize him in a six foot by nine foot cell. it is getting to the point where he cannot read. the magnifying glass he uses to decipher the print of most books is producing a reverse effect on his vision. instead of enlarging the written text, the glass shoots needles into his eyes. the pain hammers the bone behind his ears. the sluggish tide makes the pain travel into the night; it ticks off the minutes until the rude awakening of dawn . . . all right . . . all right . . . time to get up, the guards keep shouting.

solitary confinement (you be so lonely). the hard pleasure of being alone. this is the place where sam studies the complicated theoretical tracts sent to him by his friends. he reads isaac deutscher's biography on the life of trotsky and lenin about marx himself. sam's attitude towards the idea of social transformation may have been altered if a more radical and humane perspective had entered his orbit. but this hot cell is the potential site of a stabbing or a suicide. a slow crawl to the barred windows (death is perched on the sill). what he reads is better than nothing at all.

black out. the headaches are continuous. they maintain a beat from one week to the next. they mark the days by causing vertigo. the headaches force a loss of equilibrium. they are a preface to an unfolding story: the prison is about to blow.

(. . . you're a marked man, melville, a guard told him one

day in the exercise yard . . . the warden knows you're agitating among the inmates . . . and he's going to stick it to you . . .)

silence in the prison. this silence is a revolution without a face. if we ever get out of here, remind me to set the clocks back to zero. one day, we will be hopping freight trains, boarding jet airliners or slumping in a greyhound bus seat. it doesn't matter. we have gotten away from the scene of the crime. that's what counts in this age of quick successes and extended failures.

isolation opens a door to a mystery. the mind goes wild. after a few days, sam falls prey to illusions. he begins to slip. symbols repeat themselves from his subconscious. the signals bring messages in bottles from distant shores . . . jane has jumped bail and she is living underground . . . sam melville's eyes explode in their sockets.

. . . i've got keeplock's fatigue, sam melville squints at the light bulb swaying from the ceiling . . . i've got to sustain the charm against going insane.

sam has asked the prison doctor for advice, and more importantly, he wants a remedy.

. . . i can't read or write in this condition, doc, sam complains . . . and it's getting to the point where this headache of mine is interfering with physical exercise, too . . . i think it's a terminal illness.

doc sternberg is a slender and ascetic man prone to wearing brown suits. he is always burying his nose into a handkerchief soaked in eau de cologne . . . it's a habit i picked up while working in the penitentiary, he tells his wife . . . the prisoners in there are such animals . . . they have an overpowering smell that i don't want to bring home to you, darling.

. . . can you help me out, doc? sam melville asks when he is able to wrangle an appointment with the physician.

the doctor is a country surgeon. he practices medicine in the nearby villages of warsaw, batavia and attica. his methods are traditional and widely practiced. he delivers the births of children and pigs with equal fervor. he applies leeches to his patients' foreheads to extract evil thoughts. the doctor instructs mothers to rid their children of the grippe by immersing their heads in buckets of hot salt water.

. . . and if your son or daughter is masturbating, be sure to tie their hands over their heads before they go to bed, he tells parents whenever he can.

he drives an old packard, and on the days he travels to visit an ailing patient, doc sternberg can be seen for what he is: the man is an agent for a decaying rural mythologic.

the doctor describes his prison job as a disgusting task that redeems itself in two manifestations: the pay is good and the prisoners' ailments are seldom worth examining.

. . . prisoner melville, doc sternberg indulges himself with a sniff of his hanky . . . in my professional opinion, you are mistaking the symptoms of a disease with the remorse you feel due to a long stay at this correctional facility, ahem. . .

the physician brings his hands together, forming a chapel with his long fingers. he contemplates his client's medical fate with a jaundiced eye (from behind gold spectacles attached by a chain to his patrician nose).

. . . so this is the infamous sam melville, eh? the doctor snorts . . . why, he reeks of crime and the polluted jewish air of the city.

. . . i'll tell you what, prisoner melville, the doctor says . . . i'll prescribe medication for you . . . you take two of these pink tablets a day and you may rest assured the problem will cease.

. . . but what problem is that? . . . what's it called? sam asks.

. . . it's the problem that got you into this prison in the first place, young man, the country doctor snaps.

by the time sam completes the prescription, ingesting each tablet as the doctor ordered, the headaches are intensifying. they rule his body. agony is a tyrant in the kingdom of cruelty.

he spends hours crouching in a fetal position. he tries to lock out the pain by pressing his head to the wall. he is holding back a volcano . . . there isn't room for both of us, he mutters . . . either i drive out the hurt . . . or the headache will take over.

meanwhile, doc sternberg has informed warden mancusi about sam melville's plight.

. . . hello, warden? . . . yes, a good day to you, too, sir . . . this is doc sternberg . . . yes, i have been making myself scarce around these parts lately . . . listen, warden . . . i've just received prisoner 26124 in my office . . . he was seeking medical attention for an unspecified disease . . . yes, that's right . . . we are talking about the mad bomber.

the doctor's hatchet face contracts at the mouth thinking of sam. his veal-colored lips become nil when he purses them . . . what? . . . no, i was not aware of any conflict between the prisoner and corrections officer boyle.

. . . you see, warden, doc sternberg surrenders a caustic smile over the telephone . . . you understand, sir, that i am a country-bred physician trying to render you a service . . . as a rule i do not get involved with politics . . . but if i am permitted to give you my advice, the doctor goes on to say . . . i would suggest we double the dose of saltpeter in prisoner 26124's diet . . . as to eliminate the possibility of violence.

he is busy punching the walls of his cell. sam hits the concrete, drawing blood from his knuckles. he glances at the wounds in satisfaction. he sucks them dry with his tongue. behind his door (scratched with the names of convicts come and gone), he can't hear much. but judging from the quality of the vibrations coursing in the water pipes, he guesses the hour to be nightfall.

sam sits down on the bunk and relaxes. he lets his elbows rest on his knees. out of nowhere, the headache surges into his mouth, flooding it. he licks his lips and gags.

a slot in the door opens and the upper half of a brown face peers in, black eyes gleaming. the face disappears, and a few

seconds later, a plate of yellow paste is shoved into the cell.
. . . dinner is served, melville, the trustee invites . . . you'd better enjoy it while it's warm.

where did the days go? seven hundred of them were here and now they are gone . . . i am beginning to know the meaning of revolution, sam melville has written . . . it is the desire for ecstasy . . . and i think only desperation can provide it.
fourteen days later, sam is released from keeplock. to begin, he is bothered by the noise and the lights in the general population. but as the hours go on, his eyes and ears welcome a return to the main line. he grins (two weeks in solitary without cracking up). during that first day he thought he was hearing things, but he shrugs his shoulders: if he does, so what.
. . . what's the matter, melville, one of the screws taunts him . . . are you going crazy? . . . i thought i heard you flipping out the other night.
. . . what if i am going crazy? sam melville answers him . . . what can you do to stop me, huh?
the prisoner and the screw stalk each other in the cafeteria. the other men are shouting and whistling. the headache paces with increasing ferocity down his neck. a red sun is rising over the september hills of wyoming county. the heat is an inferno trapped inside his lungs. this hour may be our last. to touch the earth once more before i go. sam melville writes his final letter from attica that evening. the missive is the last key to a door (leaving the gates of attica, his words take flight back to the world) . . . i have perpetual headaches, he pencils . . . no longer taking pills.

Chapter Seventeen: Play the Music (Until the End)

. . . i stayed awake all night on september the eleventh . . . i tried to keep the brothers from losing it . . . they were running through the yard and shelters . . . some with towels and sheets wrapped around their heads, muffling their screams of fear . . . we had to drag them to the ground . . . to make them stop the hollering . . . these guys kept predicting . . . we're gonna die . . . we're gonna die . . .

. . . we knew something would happen the following morning . . . but it did nothing to change what we had accomplished . . . i am proud of my beautiful brothers . . . hard core convicts . . . murderers . . . armed robbers and pickpockets . . . punk boys and queens . . . they are innocent . . . we have kept ourselves together like free men . . . surrounded by a wilderness of loathing for our kind.

any relationship between the past and the present as described in these passages is conscious. any relationship to real life as mentioned within this story is deliberate. real life is our dream. we will do anything to get there before we die.
the act of writing is not a vehicle for simulation or recollection. nor is it an attempt to depict an idealized world. on the contrary: in this story actual people are named. the truth will be known by any means necessary. before we go to attica state prison, may i remind you of the crux to our

struggle. language is our war: all power to the imagination. let no one tell you otherwise.

on the eleventh of september, a day i always will remember, the autumn sun attacks the bald hills and melancholy valleys of wyoming county at dawn. in the little villages near the highway, the citizens are being persecuted by high temperatures. their homes are infested with black flies.

some citizens are more adventurous than others. they wait the heat out in a downtown café. an air conditioner is huffing and puffing in the back. it punctuates most conversations with a hellacious clatter. the café is dark and blessed by the shade of a towering oak tree. it is cool enough to spend a couple of hours there, and in one corner, a woman is sitting by herself at a table.

she crosses her legs at the knees. the hemline of her brown shift falls away, revealing smooth shaven legs. the fabric of the dress clings in damp patches to her stomach and breasts. she listens to a man talking at another table without looking at him. she is watching the blue smoke of his cigarette climb a rope of heat waves to the ceiling. the longer she gazes at the smoke's ascent, observing its dissipation into the torpid air, the less meaning the man's words have for her. as if on cue, he stubs the cigarette into a crystal ashtray and clears his throat. he turns to the woman. anyone can tell this isn't the first time he's laid eyes on her.

. . . they're gonna kill him . . . you know that, don't you, dora? . . . unless the governor does something fast, your johnny boy is a goner.

the man picks his nose and then lights up his second cigarette. he glances at dora from the vacuum of his eyes. he knows she is upset. she is married to a guard currently held hostage by the inmates. but this man sitting there, smoking a cigarette to calm his nerves, he may have slept with dora several times or maybe not more than once.

dora races a nervous hand over her bouffant. he can tell her fingers are stunned by the news of the convicts' rebellion. her hair is looking pitiful, he thinks, it's dirty and limp. but he can't help himself. he pulls his baseball cap over his eyes, leans back against the chair, takes in the lunchtime café crowd and caws.

. . . he's a goner no matter what happens . . . if one side doesn't kill him, the other one will.

. . . you hush up, she unloads on him . . . you're gonna wish bad luck on all of us . . . just because you want to fuck me.

an emotional plague has struck the village of attica. a disease of the spirit; it thrives on chaos and anomie. rage and despair lurk in the hearts of every woman and man. behind the byzantine architecture of attica's yellow stone walls, the nation's most alienated convicts are incarcerated, and now the worst is happening: the prisoners are revolting.

most families in the old fashioned village have a spouse or a close relative employed as a guard in the prison. in some families, the menfolk have worked the corridors of attica for several generations. their relationship to the institution is based on devotion.

insinuations, rumors, and homicide reports nourish themselves on the fear in the villagers souls. according to unofficial estimates, twenty-nine guards have been taken hostage by the rampaging inmates.

. . . they are less than men, those criminals, dora says quietly . . . they're murdering animals . . . and they'll kill anything to satisfy their blood lust . . .

america staggers on to the end of the century like a junkie whose veins are collapsing one by one. this country thinks of one thing alone (domination), and when it thinks at all, it is done with death's grin. the governor of new york is nelson rockefeller. his country estate is a mansion bordered by a park of exotic plants and imported trees. in the tranquil garden red and green hummingbirds dip their beaks to drink dew. the governor kicks off his socks and shoes to enjoy the luxurious grass carpet underfoot. he instructs the police to seize the prison.

. . . let her rip, boys, the governor chats up the police chief over the telephone . . . and get that sam melville while you're at it, will you?

the morning of september the twelfth does a strip-tease for the weatherman. a gray day is sweeping itself up from the shores of lake erie. while it searches for a place to land, it descends upon the guard towers of attica state prison. rain begins to fall in a fine mist. but as mid-morning checks in, the downpour redoubles its strength and becomes a shower.

a police helicopter hovers in the rain over the prison. the aircraft's fuselage is a vibrating carapace. its propellers rotate with the sounds of deliberate menace. the executioner is tracking its quarry . . . helicopters buzz over the city at night . . . they are soaring over the prison walls during a riot . . . the helicopters are the metal insect hunters of men.

the drama begins. the delicate velvet glove is removed from the weapon bearing fist. we are glued to our seats by the seduction of raw power. the new york state police are starting to line the walls of the prison. when the hour strikes ten, they will pour a fusillade of shotgun and rifle fire into the prisoners below. meanwhile, the helicopter sprays the yard with a blanket of white tear gas. this particular brand of gas induces nausea upon contact. men fall to their knees not to pray but to vomit.

freeze the image and look at it again: the policemen are taking their positions. their helmeted heads are bobbing up and down the stained prison walls. our pulse quickens. the noise is getting louder (it mushrooms like the death clouds of yesterday). the warm rain is turning the yard into the quicksand of mud.

the year is nineteen seventy-one. the attica state prison uprising, and its subsequent suppression will become a dress rehearsal for america's graduation into hyper-reality. when the first radio reports seep out from the smouldering ruins of the revolt, a newscaster will report . . . one man is dead who will not be missed . . . sam melville . . . the mad bomber.

. . . we weren't really surprised when the police stormed the prison . . . the negotiations between the corrections people and the prisoners had broken down the previous day . . . the word had spread that the governor himself was going to come and speak with us . . . can you imagine that? . . . nelson rockefeller standing in the exercise yard with hundreds of convicts . . . talking amidst the garbage in the rain?
. . . everyone was hoping for a few words of honesty . . . a promise made from one human being to another . . . we had our demands and the governor could start to honor them by shaking hands like a man . . . but how could we believe rockefeller would treat us fair and square?
. . . and it never did happen . . . nelson rockefeller never came to attica . . . i heard he died of something ugly later . . . what goes around, comes around, i suppose.

history has lied to us, and now is the time to intervene. it is difficult to perceive the atrocities of an american prison if you haven't been there. but given the rate of their increasing construction and occupancy, dear reader, you may have the opportunity to find out. the new words that died with the prisoners at attica are taking their turn in the gun sights of history again. the police reports said sam melville was a dangerous man. it is not for us to judge him but to let him live once more. there were parts in him that belong to every one of us. these words are associated with the growth of rebellion in the world today. they belong to sam melville who said, smiling, i am no longer depressed . . .

... the police said i came out of an improvised bunker ... a swathe of sheets and shirts ... the cops said i was running out of the bunker's entrance with a brace of molotov cocktails in my hand ... and that i was coming ... i was running to the d-yard wall to bomb them.

... i was running out of the crowd because that's where the police were aiming with their hunting rifles ... and i didn't want to get hit ... you could not believe the confusion out there ... articles of clothes caked with mud ... choruses of hoarse sobs ... men were scrambling for shelter where there was none ... fingernails digging in the dirt for salvation ... and the bullets were singing ... dum-dum bullets entered the side with a tiny hole ... and then exited through the back ... taking everything with it that wasn't already torn apart.

... a strong breeze hit us and the air turned red ... i came running like a miracle man through the gas and rain ... i felt the first hint of darkness on my skin, the cold winter to come ... it is strange how you notice the chill on a hot day ... on the day you die, all sights and sounds become clearer.

... i was approaching the walls with a couple of molotov cocktails in my hand ... and there i fell down as the bullets hit me ... death wrote out a bullet with my name on it ... and it hit me in the chest that day.

... i was thirty-five years old ... i remember what we told the world on the first day of the rebellion ... the first prison revolt in the history of humanity to be presented live on television ... we told them we are not beasts ... we are men.

his face darkens with the strength that comes from genuine anger and the knowledge of how to use it. sam melville seems ready to lose his temper and fight again. but then a shadow passes over his left shoulder. he relaxes with a visible spasm. pain takes over his eyes and they become mildly unfocussed.

... take it easy sam, death croons, easing his bony arm around the other man's neck ... you gotta stay calm ... or you'll never get to the end of the story.

bullets were ricocheting off the walls with a ping. they caused the men to duck. other shots dug into the dirt at the prisoners' feet, forcing them to jump. the pattern of the gun shots became apparent. the cops were firing into the crowd at random when they were not shooting to kill.

one man was shot in the groin. he slipped and sank into the mud with one leg twitching where his pants were ripped, torn to shreds. another man leaped backwards when his arm was blown in half. fragments of his bone spattered someone else's face who didn't even know it. prisoners were throwing up and convulsing. the gun fire was turning the ground into a palette of black mud and crimson blood. this is the juncture the police chose to enter the yard. they wanted to add a final touch to the painting they had made.

... do you want a cup of coffee, sam, or something else to drink? death asks ... i know a friendly café in attica, he chortles, forever the clown at the circus of dreams.
... yeah, i'll take a coffee without cream or sugar, sam melville says without malice.
sam's lack of anger puzzles death. the prisoner's changing moods unnerves him. he scrutinizes sam from head to foot. and sam, while his gaze is getting stronger, is still tired. he becomes self-conscious under death's stare, and he blushes.

... but i was dumb ... i didn't think they would kill us ... when the cops came down from the walls, there wasn't much we could do ... everyone huddled close to the ground ... some of the brothers refused to pull their faces out of the mud after the shooting stopped ... they were smart ... they knew something was going to happen.
... we knew the guards would be angry because of the hostages we held ... we knew they would beat us ... and

maybe force us to run a gauntlet of swinging clubs back to our cells . . . but we didn't think they would try to kill us . . . we never knew they shot some of the hostages and blamed it on us.

the police came into the yard straight from the underworld. through curtains of tear gas and mist they came. they wore long gray capes and gas masks. they shouted inside their masks but the words were impossible to discern. the state policemen were carrying shotguns, the short kind, which they held to their hips like good taxpayers out to collect a refund. the yard was a desert of men wounded and dying and scared.
three cops advanced on a man kneeling in the mud. he seemed injured or paralyzed. he tried to get to his feet, he really did. but he was so frightened, terror flared at his nostrils. the mud kept sucking at his feet. he stumbled and the three cops lighted up like a christmas tree. two of them shot the inmate in the stomach and arm. open season on the prisoners was about to commence.

unlike the living, death is acquainted with the penal institutions that dot america's countryside. no one understands the secrets of a prison better than him.
. . . i am close to most of the prisoners i meet in my travels . . . nobody cares about them and i do . . . no matter how busy i am, i will always stop to have a visit with an inmate . . . i bring them cigarettes and candy . . . my presence helps to pass the long hours of a life sentence, death says.
prisons are located in every corner of our vast nation. whenever there is a dearth of cities, that's where you can find a large and frustrated prison population. a barbed-wire compound of ramshackle wooden buildings left over from the halcyon days of world war two, that's a minimum-security prison for white-collar criminals. but do you see the fortress on the mountain? the grim castle sitting at the edge of a foreboding forest? it is not the setting of a fairy tale: no, that is

a maximum security penitentiary for unreconstructed convicts.

some place, somewhere, i don't care where, take a ride into the hinterlands, and you will discover a prison.

. . . i raised my hands . . . and i told the young con next to me to do the same . . . i don't know who he was . . . just some blood on his shirt and spittle dripping down his chin . . . hey, look out, he says to me . . . here they come.

. . . these two cops materialized in the fog . . . i tried to brace myself for the moment of impact . . . one of them pointed to me with his pistol . . . and his partner levelled a shotgun to my chest and nodded in affirmation.

. . . the thought of a woman's body passed through my mind . . . and i followed her for a second . . . i chased after her like a reflex in a nightmare . . . the nightmare is not real . . . you can swim against its pull if you want to . . . but compulsion drives you . . . it pushes you to catch up with her and learn her name and telephone number . . . and maybe kiss her.

. . . do you remember the nightmare of falling from a cliff? . . . i used to get that as a kid all of the time . . . thrown from a cliff and tumbling to the bottom . . . damn it . . . if you don't wake up, you can have a heart attack.

. . . the cop with the shotgun yelled at me . . . i couldn't hear him and i shrugged with my hands to let him know . . . but it didn't matter . . . his gas mask was covered with specks of blood . . . i saw him close one eye and take aim . . . and then he pumped two slugs into me . . . i couldn't wake up . . . i never thought the cops would try to seize the prison in an assault where thirty-nine men were killed and ninety more were wounded . . . it only took a few minutes . . . god help us.

where does a story begin if it ends with a police report? a typed and signed statement made by the new york police and sealed in a manila envelope?

the report lays on a green baize desk blotter in an office. the venetian blinds are drawn and the room is empty. the document is recorded in a cramped script. the words are made to appear smaller than the actions they describe. in this way, among others, the police hope to diminish the scale of the attica conflict.

. . . we shot sam melville like we did several others whom we suspected to be dangerous and organized . . . the order came down from the highest levels . . . the suspect was seen sprinting across the exercise yard in a suspicious and aggressive manner . . . rumors of his vaunted ability to construct incendiary devices haunted us during the three preceding days of negotiations . . . but on the fourth day, the judgment was received from the governor's mansion . . . the retribution began.

. . . sam melville was approaching the sharpshooters' roost with objects in his hands that we took to be bombs . . . his face as seen through the command post's binoculars was calm . . . his gait was rapid and vigorous . . . it was the stride of a healthy man in full control of his faculties . . . through the wounded and the dying and beyond our patience . . . the suspect was moving in an orderly fashion . . . i ordered my men to fire.

. . . i said, fire, boys, cut that fucker down . . . do you know who he is? . . . why, that's sam melville . . . the mad bomber . . . we've got to teach him a lesson.

the snipers from the state police and the investigative bureau shot the prisoner with a two-seventy winchester bullet or a thirty-two caliber shotgun shell. but after establishing the fact of this mortal wound, information becomes unavailable.

. . . further instructions include the following dictate, the police report read . . . we must make sure the history books do not remember him or the other attica prisoners . . . we must be sure our children forget the little men who died in vain.

. . . i know what you're thinking, sam, death bursts out laughing, spewing bits of a broken tooth. . . you are laboring under the assumption that nobody gives a damn!
. . . nah, i don't like the idea, sam melville replies, shaking his head as if the thought could finish off an already difficult day . . . but anyway, i'm leaving.
. . . what do you think you're doing, young man? . . . you can't walk away from me at a time like this! death exclaims.
for the second time in his life, sam melville is going to new york city.

the city is a stranger's paradise. a man is setting sail through the streets in search of his apartment. he crosses the turbulent sidewalks, never looking from left to right. once inside his room he breathes a sigh of relief; the antidote to his tension is near. privacy and unconsciousness are close at hand. (it waits for him in a brown plastic bottle under the bathroom sink.) nothing tastes better than a glass of tap water and two nembutals after long hours of work.
he pulls the curtains apart and gazes out at the night. the headlights of the cars on the bridge journey over his face. but he doesn't give himself over to fanciful thoughts because tomorrow is another day on the job and he should go to bed.
but there is no rest for the wicked. the telephone rings. the chances are five to one the voice at the other end of the line is a man with a wrong number. he glances at the clock, pondering, what the heck, it's only eleven o'clock and who knows, maybe some sweet young thing wants to talk with me. and so he snatches the receiver after the fourth ring.
. . . hello, george? the man on the telephone barks . . . this is the chief . . . i have some interesting news for you . . . hah? . . . no, i don't go out with that blonde anymore . . . listen up, george, and listen good . . . sam melville was killed at attica state yesterday . . . the police recaptured the prison . . . and i thought you might like to know because there is going to be a press conference . . . yes . . . of course you will be presented to the news reporters as the man who put the mad bomber

behind bars . . . you're going to be famous, george . . . what? . . . who do you think you're kidding? . . . you didn't know sam melville was at attica? . . . forget it, george . . . no one is going to believe you no matter what you say.

    george demmerle has the spotlight. the public eye is contemplating his fate. the hard and often precarious climb to riches and fame hasn't been easy. but now he is here to stay. he lights up a cigar after hanging up the telephone. he thinks he should go out for a drink, after all.
    but dizziness rides up his throat, sharp and creamy like toothpaste. it delivers the first wave of a nembutal rush. and it is delicious, this cotton candy web that wraps itself around his muscles. his bones are melting into pools of marrow. his arms and legs are turning slack. george's mouth opens, permitting a glimmer of saliva to teeter on his lip, and then it drops, one silver tear, spattering his pajama top.
    that's right, george. when all is said and done, you are a celebrity. you are a paper star glued to a cardboard nation.

    his eyes are glassed over. george is ready to pass out. time goes slow (he's been staring at his hand for an hour). he recognizes a knocking at his door.
    . . . who's there? he challenges.
    one fine morning, the blankets on george's bed will be saturated with perspiration and he'll wake up screaming. but right now, he says to himself, staggering to the door . . . i'm only dreaming.
    george fights the nembutal fog. he rails against its cloying hold. but he loses out and collapses to the floor. he is incapable of resisting gravity's tug. he allows his arms to be pinioned under the drug's soft weight. the knocking at the door starts again. he doesn't remember how it originated, but now that it doesn't cease, the knocking sounds like a funeral march in his ears.
    . . . who's there? he whines.

. . . sam melville, comes the refrain.
. . . go away! george demmerle cries.
. . . i can't, sam melville says . . . i've just returned.

Epilogue

a few days later, the police raided sam melville's apartment on second street. they told the world news they found a hand grenade, one nine millimeter astra pistol, a thirty caliber military issue carbine, hundreds of bullets, fifty-one dynamite blasting caps and a box of books pertaining to the study of demolition and warfare. we can only imagine the police were telling the truth or another mouthful of lies.

nothing lasts long (but the mountains and the earth). information has become a dagger on the wind; the words we hear from the amplified radios of powerful men make us doubt our strength. we cower in the shadows of the city and hope we don't get hurt. but remember: the end of history is not here. this long night filled with our most cherished dreams is not over. trouble is waiting for us at dawn (i am only beginning to make you understand that i will not play the game).

the apartment at sixty-seven second street is located across the way from an old graveyard. on this cold morning, black birds perch in the marble cemetery's trees. they watch the brown and yellow leaves fall to the ground with unconcerned eyes. these birds have seen everything (the rise and decline of autumn and its golden haze).

the disarray of grave-markers provides stepping stones for hungry pigeons pecking in the dirt. some of the monuments are ancient; the names of their patrons have eroded with time.

but on the north side of the cemetery, behind a wrought iron fence filigreed at its crest with gilded spear points, the tombs are new and well kept. a cemetery worker trudges across the graveyard lawn. he pauses to wipe his nose, and then he hefts a plastic bag of dead leaves over his shoulder with an audible grunt.

a wall of healthy green ivy is climbing the apartment building's facade. the ivy has grown tendrils over windows to the height of the fire escapes on the fourth floor. seven painted steps lead from the sidewalk to the front door. though the building wears the soot stains of the nineteenth century, the original stone carvings decorating the eaves have not deteriorated.

we are standing in front of the tallest building on the block. a window opens and a man's head pops out. even though it is noon, and the streets are dark, we are able to recognize the man at the window-sill. his name is sam melville.

today is october the fourteenth. it is the prisoner's first birthday after the uprising. the holiday finds him considering the events of the recent past. the occasion seems fitting to ask him an imperative question.

. . . this story has almost run its course, sam melville . . . where can we go from here?

he breaks open a tremulous smile. it is like the cap coming off a bottle, the carbonation sloshing over, all pink lips and white teeth. he ponders the factors that have controlled his fate: the struggle of the body to remain free of denial.

the bullets sam melville bears in his chest and lungs are a testimony. the bombs he threw were only metaphors. his militant language described the inequities of society. he is living and dying in a time and place where real life is the contest. nowadays, the war is for the language in which we speak of the man, the rebel. we are fighting the scissors of censorship that control his body and name.

on this october day, the light is peculiar. it plays itself over the brick and steel girders of the city in gray squares and bars. the weakened sun light is our sentry. the sun gives little warmth to the stone faces of the tenement buildings we see. we can look out the apartment window and observe the telephone lines magnifying their length, doubled twice by the sun (first, the object, and then, its shadow). but here comes twilight.
. . . i'd like to go beyond and see the prison doors opening . . . let the dragons fly, says he . . . if the cell that holds a man should grow dark, it is because my eyes can no longer see . . . and if my hands can't touch the cold bars, i have no reason to live . . . but if i should die without being set free, don't forget to burn down the prison in memory of me.

a child lives through his fist. we have raised the century's cry under the black and red flags calling to us. we marched towards death or liberation without regard for our safety. but we are moving to another time where the rebel lives by his or her word.
. . . i'll be back, sam melville promises . . . when life has changed and my name is cleared.
until then, samuel melville, we shall carry on without you.

life. some people celebrate and others pretend the same. time clenches its inexorable hands over human affairs. but when monday passes into friday, everyone is relieved: we are ready for the weekend. door-bells ring and invitations are extended. strangers to each other during the work week, we reacquaint ourselves with friends on saturday night.
a colleague from the old days remembers him upon a chance meeting in the street. he asks his former co-employee to attend a big dinner party at his house.
. . . don't worry, the friend reassures him warmly, saying . . .

there isn't any need to be shy, you'll have a good time.

    once inside the living-room where the party is taking place, he finds himself alone, leaning against a wall. well-dressed women and men stroll by him, almost promenading. they walk with arms linked from the kitchen to the bathroom and back to the living room where a buffet dinner is being served. the food is catered by a prestigious uptown delicatessen. it's the best caviar and anchovy paste around, everyone gushes.
    he turns to the refreshments table and assesses the spread. he doesn't know anyone at the party except the host. maybe he should eat a fragile truffle or a scrumptious pastry but he decides to help himself to a glass of fruit punch instead. he ladles the punch into a crystal goblet and drinks the fruit juice slowly. he tilts his head to let the liquid gurgle down his throat. he is relishing the cool and sweet aftertaste the juice leaves on his tongue.
    he stands there, feeling pleased with himself. his stomach agrees. his belly has accepted the ambrosia with gladness. the party is in a large brownstone, and he senses it is a privilege to be here. the furniture is tasteful. expensive tapestries cover the walls. there are quite a few young and attractive women in attendance, especially that one over there sitting on the arm of a chair. she is wearing an electric blue dress that shows everything. her black garter belt has an artificial rose pinned to it. he stares at her leg, unblinking. this might be my lucky night, he exults.
    . . . excuse me, sir, a young man with horn-rimmed glasses interrupts his reverie by tapping on his shoulder . . . excuse me . . . but did you drink any of the punch? . . . ah, i can see you already have.
    . . . yes, i did, george replies . . . and my compliments to the chef . . . it is a splendid beverage.
    . . . oh, that's good, the young man smiles. he flushes with obvious relief (his nose is glowing with embarrassment). . . because we spiked it with a lot of acid . . . and we weren't sure we told everybody who drank it . . . a simple oversight, you

can understand . . . it's so hard to plan a big party . . . something is always going wrong.

   george demmerle turns away to mask his terror. it is a candid picture of a man in flight with nowhere to hide. he muffles a high pitched whine with the palm of his hand. his voice rises to a crescendo, if not a scream. the laughter of the party goers, the glittering lights of the ersatz chandelier and the clink of glasses joined together in a toast; they lay siege to his beleaguered brain. he is hemmed in at the refreshments table by other people thirsting to drink.

   tonight is a festive event. we have come a long way (and a celebration is necessary). welcome to the party, george demmerle. it is a gift from the writer to you.

   back in tonawanda, a woman and a man are drinking in a bar. they are sitting in an upholstered booth sipping on chilled brews. we are looking at sam's mother and her boyfriend.

   the bar is called the starlight room. the harsh smell of a day old cigarette fog hits you first. a jukebox is disgorging country western songs from nashville. mirrors surround the bar, and the fan above the bartender's head blows a fringe of tinsel into the customers' faces. the only illumination in the place comes from a bank of black lights on the wall.

   . . . let's get outta here, he suggests . . . get your things together, and i'll pay the bill. he grabbed her by the hand, and she laughed.

   . . . we'll meet in the parking lot, okay? . . . and then we'll go back to the hotel. he acted as if he meant business. but she didn't believe him.

   . . . sit down beside me, she said, patting the seat next to her.

   he kneeled in front of her and pulled her dress past her thighs; he unhooked her stockings, and then he slipped his head under her taffeta dress. he luxuriated within the folds of her skirt. she stroked his back and took another swallow of her drink. she was oblivious to the stares of the other patrons lined up at the bar.

. . . it smells so good, he says, caressing her legs . . . just like the edge of a forest when the pollen goes out.

. . . hush up, you big goof, she reddened. she slapped him on the head, and he fell silent.

when he was in bed with her earlier in the evening, he thought about the city. the streaked sunsets of carbon monoxide and cirrus clouds gummed together over the sky in orange and smoke blue strips. when he moved inside her, responding to her walls grabbing and sliding with him, he was stabbed by thoughts of dying. his heart was beating so loud, blood was pounding on the tip of his tongue.

death was on the other side of the city, somewhere downtown waiting for him in a parked car. thinking about death made it troublesome for him to reach an orgasm. but she didn't mind. time was on her side, she whispered in his mouth.

he pushed into her once more. oh god, he quavered, i'm gonna keel over. and with that, he caved into her without a murmur. his breath was a pant, warming her neck. his body was harnessed by her legs. she clasped him to her breasts and smiled.

his mind is spinning as he crashes into the pillow. and she smiles. she kisses him. she tastes his sweat. she tells him she is happy, and won't he roll over to light up cigarettes for the two of them? and look at the sun, she says, lifting a hand from his shoulder to point . . . the sun is watching us. she closes her eyes and asks him to fetch her a glass of water. this text is ending exactly where it began. the miracle of life continues: with a vision.

george is peaking now. he is experiencing psychedelic anxiety (his body odor is turning strange). his hands are reverberating with a tremor, and the beautiful girl sitting on the armchair? her face is a chasm split in two. she hikes up her dress. george smiles politely and tries to avoid her eyes. he emits a keening sound . . . i think i'm in trouble, he says to himself.

things fall apart. the guests at the party are staring at him, motioning with their lips as if he were an idol in a wax museum. the host comes up to him and asks, are you okay, george? . . . some of my friends say you're acting funny.

the question is like a coffin to george . . . he looks into the open box. flies are crawling over the deceased's head . . . george recognizes himself in his host's drunken eyes, and he starts to shudder . . .

the dead man stands up in his coffin and walks away. the flesh is pulled from the bone. the skeleton leaves behind a puddle of blood and skin. bricks and plaster are cascading from the ceiling. the floorboards buckle and groan. outside, buildings are sinking into the ground one by one.

the world stands still at the center of a storm. negligees are ripped from the women. jockey shorts are yanked from the men. but no sooner are the guests naked and ready to face each other, than gravity pulls apart their limbs. feet are torn from the leg. heads are wrung by the neck.

. . . listen, george . . . the women are starting to complain . . . do you think you could get up from under the table? . . . good . . . good . . . that's better . . . god, man, look at you . . . you've made a mess . . . jesus, i can't believe it . . . right in your pants.

skyscrapers are crumbling into dust, raising geysers of steel, glass and oily fire. underneath the cobblestones is the soil (and the bones of men), and beneath the dirt, the core of the earth is bubbling in a molten river. down here, molecules are extracted from the air. oxygen is stripped from carbon. and after their separation from the neutrons, the atoms, they die. nothing is left. only his screaming in the river. george demmerle claws at his eyes with a fistful of fingers. darkness is everywhere.